Runaway

Tyndale House Publishers, Inc. • Carol Stream, Illinois

STARLIGHT

1

Animal Rescue

Runaway

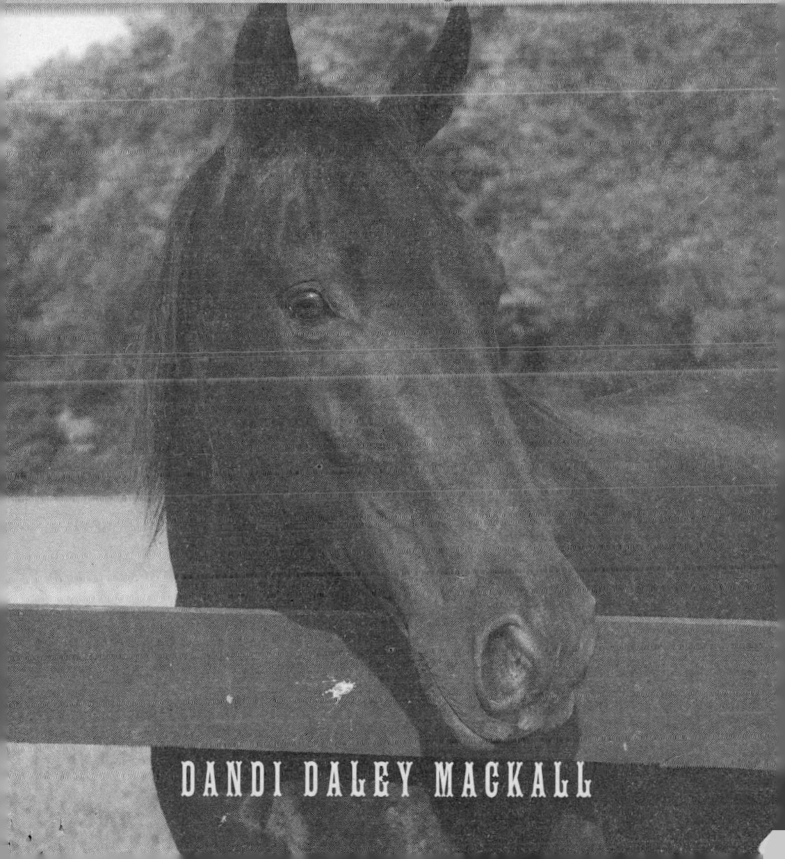

DANDI DALEY MACKALL

Visit Tyndale's exciting Web site at www.tyndale.com

You can contact Dandi Daley Mackall through her Web site at
www.dandibooks.com

TYNDALE and Tyndale's quill logo are registered trademarks of
Tyndale House Publishers, Inc.

Runaway

Designed by Jacqueline L. Nuñez

Edited by Stephanie Voiland

Scripture quotations are taken from the *Holy Bible*, New Living
Translation, copyright © 1996, 2004, 2007 by Tyndale House
Foundation. Used by permission of Tyndale House Publishers, Inc.,
Carol Stream, Illinois 60188. All rights reserved.

ISBN-13: 978-1-4143-1268-2
ISBN-10: 1-4143-1268-7

Printed in the United States of America

14 13 12 11 10 09 08
 7   6   5   4   3   2   1

WHEREVER WE'RE GOING, I won't be staying. That much I can promise. I've run away seven times—never once *to* anything, just *away from*. Maybe that's why they call me a "runaway" and not a "run-to."

The way I figure it, these "ideal placements" by Chicago's social services never add up to much. And anyway, so far, my life has been subtraction. Two parents and a brother and me. Take away one brother, and that leaves two parents and me. Take away one parent, and that leaves one parent and me. Take away another parent, and that leaves me,

Dakota Brown, age almost 16, trying not to wonder what it will be like when I'm the one taken away.

Bouncing in the backseat of the social worker's car—the front seat has too many papers and folders *about* me to fit the real me in it—I decide it's time for a list. I love lists. You can take a mess like Ms. Social Worker has going for her in the front seat and, in a few minutes, turn it into a list that fits on a single sheet of paper. Lists bring things under control. *My* control.

I take my list-book out of my backpack and turn to a clean page. Glancing in the rearview mirror, I catch the frown of concentration on the social worker's face. She's too busy trying to get us out of Chicago traffic to worry about what I'm doing in the backseat.

I know her name is Ms. Bean, but in my head I keep thinking of her as "the social worker" because things are easier that way. She's not a bad person, and I'm not trying to get her into trouble or anything. But because I'm so good at what I do—running away—I'm bound to make her look pretty lousy at what she does. She thinks she's driving me to my

2

new foster family, where I'll live happily ever after and forever be a pleasant anecdote for her to share with friends and family and future fosters everywhere.

Poor Ms. Social Worker. She is doomed to fail. The State of Illinois has not invented a foster family from which I, Dakota Brown, cannot escape.

In my list-book, I form an action plan.

THE PLAN:

A. Pay attention to the route leading to my new location. It is also my route out.

B. Control reaction to new setting. It's important that the social worker believes I like my new digs.

C. Headache. This will be my medical weapon of choice, the only complaint I'll voice, my one excuse to get out of whatever needs getting out of.

D. Observe. Knowledge is power.

E. Never cry. At least, never let them see you cry.

F. Never get angry. (Yeah, right.) Don't let them see the anger.

G. Never "confide," as the social worker likes to call it.

H. Be friendly, but do not make friends.

"Dakota, what are you writing?" Ms. Bean asks.

"Sorry." I close my list-book and flash a smile to the rearview mirror.

"Don't be sorry," she says, smiling back at the mirror. This action makes her come up too fast on the little sports car in front of us.

"Ms. Bean!" I shout.

She slams on the brakes, forcing the car behind us to do the same. Horns honk. "I hate traffic," she admits.

I wonder how she ended up in Chicago when she hates traffic so much. But I don't ask. My mind reaffixes the *Ms. Social Worker* label, and I stare out the window.

Ms. Bean is not the clichéd social worker. She's a stylish, 24-year-old college graduate with light red hair, funky earrings, and clothes I wouldn't mind wearing myself. I know she's engaged. But other than the fact that she's a lousy driver, I don't know much else about her. That's the way I like it.

4

I lean back and close my eyes, hoping she'll drop the subject of my writing notebook, her driving, and everything else. After a minute, I open my eyes and stare out the window again. Cars whiz by all around us. Every car window is closed. Heat rises from the pavement between the lanes. Even with the air-conditioning blasting, I can smell Chicago, a mixture of tar, exhaust fumes, and metal.

The social worker slams on her brakes again, but I can't see any reason for it this time.

"Sorry about that," she mutters. Maybe to me. Maybe to the guy behind her, who rolls down his window enough to scream at her.

"Don't stop writing on my account, Dakota," she says. "Unless it makes you carsick. It always makes me carsick."

I'm thinking that if I get carsick, it will have more to do with her driving style than it does with my writing style. But Rule #11 on my "How to Handle Social Workers" list is "Don't criticize. It puts them on the defensive."

I say, "You're right, Ms. Bean. I really shouldn't write while I'm in the car."

"My sister is a journalist," Ms. Bean tells me.

It's more information than I care to know. I don't want to picture her as a person, with a newspaper-writing sister.

"Charlotte has a mini recorder she carries with her everywhere," the social worker continues. "Instead of writing notes, she talks into that recorder, even when she's driving. My dad keeps telling her not to record and drive, but she won't listen."

She hits her horn when someone changes lanes right in front of her without signaling.

"How far out of Chicago is this place?" I ask.

"Nice?"

I know this is the name of the town they're dragging me to, but it takes a second to register. "Yeah. Nice," I say. "Only are you sure they don't pronounce it 'Niece,' like that city in France?" Both cities are spelled the same, but I'm guessing the similarities end there.

"That would make sense," she admits. "But no. You'll be living in Nice, Illinois." She giggles. "And going to Nice High. And I'm sure you'll be a nice resident of Nice."

I manage to smile, although I can only imagine how old this play on names must get.

I'm already feeling not so nice about it. "So, are we getting close?"

"It's still a good ways," Ms. Bean answers. "The board thought a rural home might be a nice change for you." She smiles, then lets the "nice" thing fade without comment.

Neither of us says anything, so her last words bang around in my head. The board thought a rural home would be a nice change? The board doesn't know me well enough to know how ridiculous it is to think a rural home would be just the ticket for Dakota Brown. The "ticket" for me is a one-way ticket out of there.

"Are you writing a book?" Ms. Bean asks.

"No," I answer, hoping she'll leave it alone.

"No? A letter, maybe?"

Those files scattered all over the front seat have enough information on me that she should know there's nobody in the world I'd write a letter to. "It's just lists," I say to get her off my case.

"Like a shopping list?"

"Just a list," I answer, trying not to let her see that this conversation is getting to me.

"Like what, for example?" Ms. Bean can turn into a little kid sometimes. She reminds me of this girl, Melody, who was in a foster home in Cicero with me for two months. Melody would grab on to a question and not let it go until she shook an answer out of you.

"Read me one, will you, Dakota?" she begs.

I'm pretty sure Ms. Bean will keep asking me about lists until I either read her one or get so angry I won't be able to keep up my cheerful act. That, I don't want.

I open my list-book and flip through dozens of lists until I come to a social worker–friendly list. "Okay . . . here's a list of five cities I want to visit one day." This is a real list I've made, but I have a hundred cities on it. Not five.

"That's awesome!" she exclaims. "Which cities, Dakota?"

"Paris, Vienna, Rome, Moscow, and Fargo." I stop and close the notebook before she can peek in the rearview mirror at the next list, because it looks like this:

TOP 8 CITIES I NEVER WANT TO SEE AGAIN
  1. Elgin, IL
  2. Evanston, IL

3. Aurora, IL
4. Glen Ellyn, IL
5. Kankakee, IL
6. Cicero, IL
7. Chicago, IL
8.

Ms. Bean was my social worker in only the last two cities, but she's got files on me from the other five. So she'd pick up on this list right away and make a big deal of it if she saw it.

I wait until she's totally confused and trying to study her map while avoiding crashing into trucks. Then I open my list-book and fill in that blank by #8 of the cities I never want to see again.

When I'm sure she's not looking, I write in big letters:

Nice, IL

WHEN THE SOCIAL WORKER first told me about their big plan to exile me to rural Illinois, I pictured a cross between Old MacDonald's farm and *Little House on the Prairie*. It was all I could do not to bolt right then and there. The thought of sleeping in the same place as cows and chickens and whatever made me swear to myself that I wouldn't spend a single night down on the farm.

My first action plan didn't look like the one I have now. Instead, I made a list of ways I could leave the farm the same day I arrived. I thought about breaking out into fits of sneezing the minute I set foot on the farm and not stopping until I was back in the city. I considered faking a horrible headache and making Ms. Bean call 911. I even thought about hiding in the trunk of her car.

Then I e-mailed Neil to see which plan I should go with. Neil Ramsey is this guy I've known for two years. We ended up at the same "home" when I was in between fosters. Neil hasn't had a foster family since he was 11. So he'd been in the "holding tank home" longer than anybody. Basically, the home was an orphanage for the kids who fell through the foster care cracks. Neil ruled the place.

Right away, Neil showed me the ropes. I was only there a month, but we've kept in touch through e-mail. Ms. Bean and the social service people get all worked up about Neil being a bad influence. But he's not. And we're not, like, boy-friend and girlfriend or anything. He just knows the score, knows how to play the game. Neil says nobody in the whole world cares if people like us live or die, or what happens to us in between. So we've got to stick together.

Anyway, Neil shot down every getaway plan I came up with. My whole entire list. He said I had to use my head, and he was right. Which is why I came up with my new plan to make everybody think I'm the good little foster girl. Then, when they're least expecting it, Neil's going to help me bust out of there. For good this time.

"Dakota?" Ms. Bean glances at me in the rearview mirror. "You're so quiet, honey. Are you worried?"

"Maybe a little," I admit, only because it will get me what I want: more information. I've met the family a few times, of course, but mostly we talked about me. All I know about Mr. and Mrs. Coolidge is that they smile a lot and don't look much like their son, Hank, who's almost 16 but already a head taller than his dad.

"Could you tell me more about the Coolidges?" I ask. Knowledge is power. That's what Neil says.

"Sure!" She changes lanes without signaling. "I'll start with Dr. Coolidge. Ann."

It's still hard for me to believe Ann Coolidge is a real doctor. She's short and shaped like a bowling pin. Plus, she's as scattered as pick-up-sticks.

"Dr. Coolidge is chief oncologist in Nice Samaritan Hospital, so she has to drive in to work every day. But Mr. Coolidge is almost always at the farm."

"The farm's not in Nice?" I ask, trying to hide my panic. The farther from civilization, the more complicated it's going to be to get out.

"I suppose it's 20 minutes to town. No longer than a half hour on the school bus."

I bite my tongue so I won't scream, "School bus!" Instead, I take a deep breath and remind myself that I won't be there when school starts.

Ms. Bean continues filling me in on life down on the farm. "Dr. Ann could work in any cancer unit in the United States, if she wanted to. You'll just love Ann once you get to know her. She–" Ms. Bean stops, as if searching for the right words. "She's one of a kind."

That much I'd already gathered.

"I'm sorry you didn't get to spend more time with the family before moving in. Don't you love Chester Coolidge, though?" Ms. Bean says.

I don't answer. The guy's totally friendly, but he makes me think of Popeye the Sailor Man–bald, big arms, stocky.

"Chester is a part-time fireman, but mostly he oversees the animals." She shakes her head, like she's an inch from laughing. I don't ask. "Did I tell you the farm's called Starlight Animal Rescue?"

"Yeah."

"So sometimes there are a lot of animals to care for. And the kids, of course."

"I thought they only had Hank." And Hank is no "kid." I pegged him for 18 when I first met him.

"I did tell you that you weren't the only foster child," Ms. Bean reminds me.

Fosters don't count, although I know better than to share this thought with her.

"There's Wes," she continues. "He's 14 and has had a rough time of it. And Katharine. She's been with the Coolidges about two years, since she was nine. They're in the process of adopting her."

Nine. That's how old I was when my dad died and I went to live with my first foster family. I can't help wondering what this kid Katharine has that would make somebody want to adopt her. Nobody ever wanted to adopt me.

"Did you get to talk to Hank much?" Ms. Bean asks, turning on the windshield wipers, although it's still sunny.

"He asked if I liked horses." Meeting foster families always feels like auditioning for a play. And the lines are lame.

"Hank is a wizard with horses," she says. "No, not *wizard* . . . *whisperer*! He's a horse whisperer, although he'll deny it. But people bring abused horses to the farm, and Hank fixes them right up. The Coolidges are all about animals. Chester has a brother in Ashland, Ohio, and they call his son, Hank's cousin, 'Catman' because he's so good with cats. Catman and his friend Winnie operate a pet helpline. Hank e-mails Winnie for horse advice. He calls her 'Winnie the Horse Gentler.'"

I'm trying to listen, but Ms. Bean's turn signal has been on so long that it's driving me crazy. I'm thinking about telling her to turn it off when she jerks the wheel to the right, crosses a lane of traffic, and takes an exit.

"Almost missed our exit," she announces.

She stops the car at the top of the exit ramp and consults the map. "Never could read

16

these things," she mutters. After a minute, she tosses the map, shrugs, and turns left.

I'm thinking she made the wrong guess because we pass nothing but trees and fields for miles.

Then, as if we've been stranded in the desert and have finally stumbled onto civilization, Ms. Bean shouts, "Look! Nice!"

If this is civilization, then it got lost in a time machine. It's like time warped somewhere between Chicago and here. We've zoomed back in time to 1950. All-American boys are riding bikes along Main Street. Plump, gray-haired ladies sit on front porches, surrounded by pink and red flowers. More flowers line cracked sidewalks and pool in circles around the trees.

We drive past a big sign that reads, "Welcome to Nice! Nice to have you!" The sign needs paint.

"Isn't it beautiful?" Ms. Bean exclaims. "Frank and I would love to live in a town like this after we're married."

"Uh-huh," I say because I'm having trouble getting my breath.

"Look!" She points left, and the car moves with her, crossing the centerline. Nobody honks at her. "See that white stucco building? The Made-Rite has the best sandwiches in the state. Chester and Ann took me there the last time I came to Nice."

She's obviously waiting for me to say something. "Good sandwiches, huh?" I have no idea what a "made-rite" sandwich could be and even less of a desire to find out.

"Awesome! Chester said his parents used to take his brother and him to this very restaurant when they were kids, but only for special occasions. The Coolidges still celebrate birthdays at the Made-Rite." She smiles into the rearview mirror. "When's your birthday, Dakota? I know I have it here somewhere." She starts to rummage through the folders scattered across the front seat. The car wanders into the wrong lane.

"July 4," I say quickly, before she crashes into a mailbox.

"Well, of course. How could I forget? Less than two weeks away. I'll bet you can celebrate at the Made-Rite and then watch Nice fireworks on your birthday."

I think I'm going to be sick.

Neither of us talks as she tries to pass a

truck on a barely two-lane blacktop road. As soon as she succeeds in passing, she slams on the brakes and turns onto a gravel road. White dust kicks up like dry fog. "Won't be long now."

I prepare myself. I've been through this enough times. Everyone is super sickly sweet on Drop-Off Day. I just want to get it over with.

We bounce off the gravel road and onto a dirt lane. It's a long driveway, ending at a standard grayish farmhouse.

"We're here!" Ms. Bean exclaims, as if I hadn't guessed. Then she slams on her brakes.

In front of us, blocking the drive, is a scene I'd never have expected on Drop-Off Day, not even in inner-city Chicago. In front of us, Hank is screaming at a kid half his size. The kid is wired, yelling back and looking like he could take Hank with one hand tied behind his back. At their feet, a giant German shepherd is barking and lunging at the shorter kid, while a shriek fills the air, as if from an invisible girl gone stark-raving mad.

Every family I've lived with, even the good ones, bent over backwards to impress social workers. All of us kids had to be on our best behavior when the social worker showed up. So if this is the family's best behavior, I am in serious trouble.

Three

I THINK FAST AND LOCK MY DOOR. Ms. Bean hasn't moved since she stopped for the "show" in the driveway. Even with the windows up, I can hear the guys yelling at each other. But I can't make out the words, maybe because of that eerie screaming in the background.

Cautiously, I crack open my window for better eavesdropping.

"If it's such a big deal, *you* do it!" the shorter kid shouts. He's dressed like half the guys I know in Chicago—black cap backwards, black T-shirt, low-riding jeans.

"Why should *I* do it?" Hank waves his arms like he's trying to fly.

"Your farm," the kid answers, crossing his arms and sticking out his chin.

I have to admit that there's something kind of cool about watching two people yell at each other . . . when one of them isn't me.

"Well, you live here!" Hank shouts. "I do 10 times as much work around this place as you do."

"So? You wanna fight about it?" The kid raises his fists.

Out of nowhere comes stocky Chester Coolidge. All that's missing is the opened can of spinach and the Popeye theme song.

This is getting good.

Mr. Coolidge wedges himself between the boys. "Enough."

They stop but keep glaring at each other over Mr. Coolidge's bald head.

Ms. Bean springs into action. She opens her door, but I notice that she keeps one foot in as she stands and waves. "Hello? We're here!"

I hop out of the car and walk toward them because I don't want to miss the look on

Coolidge's face when he sees he's been caught by the social worker.

"Hey! Great! You made it!" He waves and smiles, as if he's not embarrassed or flustered at all. As if we didn't just catch him breaking up a fight between his bio son and his foster son—a huge social worker no-no. "Hang on a minute. Be right there!" he calls.

"That's Wes," Ms. Bean whispers, pointing to the short African American kid with the barking dog.

At least the invisible girl has stopped screaming.

"I'm not mowing!" Wes snaps. The big dog barks louder, its tail wagging. "Let 'big brother' Hank do it. It's *his* lawn. Not mine. Or *you* do it yourself."

Hank starts to say something but stops with one look from Popeye.

"I'd be pleased to mow the lawn, Wes," Mr. Coolidge says. "In truth, I enjoy mowing. Lets you see where you've been and where you must go." He reaches over and strokes the big dog's head. The dog stops barking.

Wes narrows his eyes, and I think he's going to ask what the catch is. I would. Then

23

he sticks out his lip in that street-smart pose. "Yeah? That's just fine then. You like mowing so much, go for it. 'Cause I'm not doing it." He smirks at Hank, like he's won the argument.

"It's just a shame you won't have the opportunity to mow again for a whole week, unless we get more rain." Mr. Coolidge glances up at the sky.

"Yeah, that's real bad news, all right," Wes says with admirable sarcasm.

"I'm truly sorry about that, Wes," Mr. Coolidge says. He seems so sincere.

Wes looks thrown off by Mr. Coolidge. "What are you sorry about? I'm getting me a week off."

Mr. Coolidge nods. "This is true." He sighs. "No mowing. No TV. No Internet. No computer games."

"What are you talking about?" Wes demands. The dog nudges his arm and barks twice.

"You know how it works, Wes," Mr. Coolidge replies, his voice even, with that touch of regret. "Package deal—chores and privileges. I'm just sorry your main chore only comes around once a week. Means you don't get the opportunity to employ the package for an entire week."

Wes huffs and shuffles his feet. "Fine!" He pulls a leash out of his pocket and snaps it to the collar of the barking dog. "Come on, Rex. Let's get out of here."

Wes looks so angry stomping across the yard that I wonder if he'll just keep on walking and never come back. The four of us stare after him—Hank and his dad, me and the social worker.

"Isn't Wes something?" Mr. Coolidge observes. He says it as if Wes has just won a trophy for walking old ladies across the street.

"Well," Ms. Bean begins, "I suppose he does have a long way to go."

"That boy is doing great!" Mr. Coolidge smiles straight at the social worker. "Did you see the way he walked that dog without even being told? No way he would have done that a month ago." He turns to Hank. "Right, Son?"

"That's for sure," Hank says. He doesn't sound angry anymore. If I didn't know better, I'd think there was a sort of pride, or admiration, in his voice too. "That dog loves Wes."

Mr. Coolidge is animated now, like a

cartoon Popeye. "Rex is the best thing that ever happened to Wes. That dog knows when Wes is getting angry before any of us, before Wes himself. It's like Rex is a smoke detector for Wes's fiery anger. Did you see the way the dog barked to warn Wes about his temper? Wes didn't listen this time, but still."

I thought it was strange that the dog barked only at Wes, not at Hank or Mr. Coolidge.

"And Wes is the best thing that could have happened to Rex," Hank adds. "You should have seen that poor dog when Wes found him, scrawny and battered. Somebody dumped him out on the road."

"That's terrible!" Ms. Bean exclaims.

"Wes nursed him back to health," Hank continues. "It was the first time we'd seen that soft side of him. They've been a team ever since."

I've never had a pet. But it makes me crazy when I see people picking on animals just because they can. "Did you ever find out who hurt the dog?" I ask.

Hank shakes his head. "We almost never do. People dump all sorts of pets out here. They know we'll take care of them."

"Remember that *101 Dalmatians* movie?" Mr. Coolidge bursts into a laugh that sounds like tree branches cracking in a hurricane.

Hank grins. "Every time they show that movie, we know we're in for trouble. I think we've ended up with almost 101 dalmatians dumped on our doorstep. Kids beg for a spotted puppy, but after a few weeks of spotted carpets, parents are ready to get rid of the pets, and kids have moved on to the next movie."

"Chihuahuas!" Mr. Coolidge lets out that laugh again.

Ms. Bean glances at me and looks like she's about to split her sides trying not to laugh.

"Taco Bell commercial," Hank explains. "We still get collies when they come out with a new *Lassie* movie and retrievers when they show that other movie . . . what is it? Oh yeah, *Air Bud*. There's a Saint Bernard movie they run every now and then too. Man, I hate pet movies."

I glance around, expecting to see hundreds of Chihuahuas, dalmatians, retrievers, and Saint Bernards roaming the property.

As if he's reading my mind, Mr. Coolidge says, "We manage to adopt out nearly all our charges, sooner or later." He turns toward me and claps his hands. "Dakota Brown! Welcome!"

"Thanks?" I glance at Ms. Bean and wonder if hiding in her trunk might not be such a bad idea after all.

"Miami phoned to apologize deeply." Mr. Coolidge says this to me and looks like he's waiting for a response.

"Miami?" I've never been there and can think of no reason why the city would want to apologize to me.

"Ha!" He lets out that crack of laughter. "*My* Annie! Not *Miami*! My Annie phoned to say how sorry she is that she couldn't make it home in time to greet you."

It still sounds like *Miami* when he says it. I shrug.

"She promises to make it up to you, and Miami always keeps her promises."

"Bags in the car?" Hank asks, moving toward the trunk.

"Thank you, Hank," Ms. Bean says, close on his heels.

I have only two suitcases. Ms. Bean gets my pack out of the backseat. When I hear the clunk of the trunk slamming shut, I shudder. This is all getting too real.

"Will you stay for dinner, Ms. Bean?" Mr. Coolidge asks.

There's a part of me that's screaming, *Yes! Please! Please stay! Don't go!* Not that I'm such a Ms. Bean fan or anything. Maybe it's the old "misery loves company" thing. I'm miserable, and I don't want to be left here alone.

The social worker glances at her watch. "I wish I could. But I have to get back to the city. I can't believe how late it is. It took me a lot longer getting here than I thought it would." She turns to me. "Are we forgetting anything, Dakota?"

Yes! Me!

I shrug.

"I'll take your bags on in," Hank says.

I stare after him as he struggles toward the old farmhouse. I've barely glanced at it, as if it doesn't have anything to do with me. But now my stuff is going in there. And I'm supposed to go with it. The house is so not me. Too *Nice.* Too old-fashioned. Too old, period. The trees spreading branches across the steep, sloped roof must be a hundred years old.

"Dakota?" Ms. Bean says this like she's already said it a few times.

I should be used to this by now, shouldn't I? This is my eighth foster stopover. I don't have a home to be homesick for. Besides, it's not like Ms. Bean and I are family, or even friends. It's not like I'll miss her. I almost wish that I would miss her. Then I'd have a reason for the empty feeling in my gut right now.

Maybe it's just that every time I'm dumped somewhere new, it hits me hardest that I've got nobody old to miss.

FOUR

"DAKOTA?" Ms. Bean comes over and stands beside me. "Are you all right?"

"Sure," I say. And as I say it, I know it's one of the biggest lies I've ever told. Not one of the worst, but definitely one of biggest. Might as well follow it with another one. "I was just admiring the farmhouse."

Mr. Coolidge blushes. "Well, it's nothing fancy, but we like it."

We walk back to the car together. Mr. Coolidge jogs ahead to open the door for Ms. Bean.

She seems surprised. "Why, thank you.

I'm not sure I can remember the last time a gentleman opened the door for me."

Mr. Coolidge looks just as surprised by this news as Ms. Bean was to have her door opened for her. "Maybe you should bring that fiancé of yours with you next time," he suggests. "I'd like to have a little talk with that fellow."

"I . . . I'll have to think about that," she replies.

"Say!" Mr. Coolidge exclaims. "You should bring him out for the Fourth of July! We're going to the Made-Rite. It's Hank's birthday."

She laughs. "It's Dakota's birthday too. What a coincidence!"

"No coincidences," Mr. Coolidge says. "Only God appointments."

It's not the first time I've heard him mention God. I get the feeling God's a big deal with the Coolidges.

"Two birthdays, plus the birth of our nation?" Ms. Bean seems to be mulling this over. "Plus the Made-Rite? I'll talk to Frank."

"Tell him he's more than welcome to celebrate with our birthday boy and girl," Mr. Coolidge assures her.

I could tell them that this birthday girl

won't still be around on July 4. But I wouldn't want to spoil their plans.

Or mine.

Ms. Bean starts the car, then sticks her head out the window and fixes me with a look so intense that I have to bite my lip. "Dakota, if you need anything, call me." She rummages through her purse and hands me her business card. "Now, call anytime you feel like it. Okay?"

I take the card and notice her e-mail address. It's the perfect opportunity to ask what I've wanted to ask since I got here. I turn to Mr. Coolidge. "Could I use your computer? No long-distance charge for e-mail." I have to be able to e-mail Neil. And the sooner, the better, as far I'm concerned. I need a plan. I need a list.

"You can use the phone to call Ms. Bean whenever you like," Mr. Coolidge offers.

I fight down panic. "You don't have the Internet out here?"

He chuckles, but not the limb-cracking laugh. "We do. Computer's in the kitchen."

It's a weird place for a computer, but at least they have one. "Great. Thanks."

Mr. Coolidge and I watch Ms. Bean's car drive away in a puff of dust, as if it's vanished. When she's totally out of sight, I realize that something's humming. A low buzz comes and goes, like somebody messing with the volume on a station that won't come in.

"Crickets," Mr. Coolidge says, although I haven't asked. "And . . . hear that?"

Above the cricket buzz is a tapping.

"Woodpecker," he says.

"I don't think I've ever heard a wood-pecker before," I admit.

"One of the good Lord's best gifts," he says. "I can feel that tapping in my soul. Can't you? God's knocking at the soul."

I have no idea how to answer that one.

"Cat!" Mr. Coolidge shouts.

I glance around for one but don't see any. A few yards from the house is a barn that looks like it was made out of the same wood as the house. A hand-painted sign above the door reads *Starlight Animal Rescue*. But I don't see a cat.

"Come down and meet Dakota," Mr. Coolidge commands.

I should be surprised that he talks to invisible cats. Somehow I'm not.

"Don't just sit up in that tree and watch," Mr. Coolidge shouts in the general direction of the treetop behind me. "Come down and introduce yourself to our new arrival. You can show her around."

"Seriously," I say, sidestepping toward the house, more determined than ever to find that computer, "not such a huge fan of cats. I can show myself around."

He laughs. "K-a-t, not c-a-t."

"Right," I say, knowing it's healthiest to agree with crazy people. I read this somewhere once.

He waves over my head again.

I spin around in time to see a little girl drop down from the tree. That explains the invisible-girl shriek I heard when we first drove into this place. I'd forgotten about that one. The girl is thin and so white it's like I can see through her. Everything about her looks fragile. She reminds me of an angel tree-topper, except for one striking difference: her hair. It's the brightest orange red I've seen since that Orphan Annie movie. The way it bushes out around her face makes her head look three times too big for her shoulders.

She walks toward us soundlessly, like a forest nymph, wearing a sleeveless white shirt and jean shorts. I can see the tiny purple veins in her arms.

"Kat," Mr. Coolidge says, "this is Dakota Brown. Dakota, this is Katharine Hall."

I try to keep from staring at her frizzy orange hair. I can just imagine the kind of teasing she'd get in the schools I've gone to. "Hey," I say in her general direction.

She smiles, showing a row of tiny white teeth.

"Kat," Mr. Coolidge says, "I need to do Wes's mowing. Will you show Dakota around?"

She nods. When she starts toward the house, she says something in a soft voice. I'm not sure, but I think she said, "I'll show you your bed."

I follow her to the house. The lawn is bumpy and tufted, with half-gnawed dog bones here and there. Something smells good, like flowers or rain. Or maybe country. What would I know?

She keeps glancing back at me, as if making sure I'm coming. "You're even prettier than they said you were."

"What?" I'd like to know who said I was pretty. Or who said I wasn't as pretty as I am. Not that I think I'm ugly. I just don't think I'm especially pretty—dark complexion, black hair, brown eyes some say are black. I could pass for Native American, and sometimes I tell people that's what I am.

Kat holds the screen door open so I can go in. "This is the living room."

I scan the room filled with stuffed furniture—a couch with a blanket over the back, an easy chair, a short couch—and a small TV. It would all be pretty ordinary, except for the animals. They're everywhere. Cat curtains, horse wallpaper, two dog portraits on the wall. Across the living room is a dining area with a big table and mismatched chairs, some with dog cushions, others with cat cushions.

I break out in a sweat, but I think it's because of the room temp, and not my raging panic. "Kat, is it always this hot in here?"

"Just in summer," she answers.

I can't tell if she's being funny on purpose or not. A quick look around shows long windows wide open. "Don't you have air-conditioning?"

She doesn't answer. "This way." Kat points to a big kitchen off the hallway. There's a wooden butcher block in the center and counters on three sides. "You don't have to ask when you want something to drink or eat."

"That's good," I say, my eyes searching for the computer. I spot it sitting on a small desk between the kitchen and the dining area. I'm dying to get online and write Neil, but I don't want Orphan Annie watching over my shoulder.

"Up here!" Kat's halfway up a narrow stairway that leads to the second floor. "Bedrooms are up here. Mom and Dad's is down the hall."

Mom and Dad's?

If this kid weren't so fragile and shy, I'd warn her about counting chickens that may never hatch. She's setting herself up for a fall, calling the Coolidges Mom and Dad before things are official. Adoption is a tricky business.

I follow her into a medium-size room with two single beds and one dresser. I've had worse rooms. Once I shared a room this size with three other girls, who were known as "the crier," "the screamer," and "the snorer." I was "the runner."

The only thing wrong with this picture is the pictures. Cat posters on the walls, cat curtains, cat trinkets on the dresser.

"You really like cats, huh?" Both beds sport identical cat bedspreads.

"I love cats," she admits. "Do you know Catman?"

"Hank's cousin, right? Nope."

"Catman knows everything there is to know about cats," Kat explains.

"You don't say." I'm barely listening to her as I size up the windows in this room. No locks. Two stories, but one big, climbable tree outside the far window. Easy exit.

"Yeah," Kat continues. "Whenever I have a question about cats, I e-mail the Catman, and he always knows the answer."

Something moves on one of the bed pillows, and I see it's a real cat, a kitten that was blending in with all the bedspread cats. It's small, white, scraggly, and pretty ugly.

"This is Kitten," Kat says, tiptoeing toward the scroungy cat. She reaches the bed and sits down without jiggling the pillow. She just sits there, her hands in her lap.

The kitten eyes her, then backs away.

"Kitten is shy," Kat whispers, without looking at it. "It took three weeks to get her to come inside the house."

Slowly, the kitten creeps toward Kat. She waits. She's so still I don't think she's breathing. Finally, the kitten rubs against her leg. Then it puts one paw on her leg. Then the other. After another minute, it settles on her lap, and Kat strokes its matted fur.

"You can have either bed you want," Kat tells me.

I choose the bed she and the cat aren't sitting on. Fine with me. Closer to the escape window.

There's a commotion outside. I hear brakes squeal, a car door slam. Then voices are shouting. Mr. Coolidge's cry comes through the open window: "Miami! I missed you!"

A woman's cry matches his. "My Chester! Come here to me!"

"Is that Dr. Coolidge?" I ask.

Kat nods. "That's Mom."

"How long has she been gone?" I ask. I can still hear them declaring how much they've missed each other.

Kat laughs. It sounds like purring. "Mom

left early this morning. They do this every day though, even when she doesn't go in early. You'll get used to it."

Thunderous footsteps sound on the stairs. "Dakota? Where are you?" Annie Coolidge's curly brown hair appears at the top of the stairs. Before I can answer her, she jogs into the bedroom. "Please forgive me for not being here when you arrived! Surgery. Still, no excuse."

"That's okay, Dr. Coolidge," I answer.

"Annie," she says. "You're not going to go around calling me Dr. Coolidge. I'm sure not calling you Dr. Brown." She seems shorter than when I met her in Chicago. And rounder. I can't imagine being wheeled into the hospital and finding out she's my surgeon. She's probably a great doctor, like Ms. Bean said. She just so does not look the part.

She glances at Kat, who's still petting the kitten. "Hi, Kat. Hi, Kitten."

"Hi, Mom," Kat answers. "Doesn't Dakota look good in here?"

Dr. Coolidge—Annie—narrows her eyes at Kat. "Katharine Elizabeth?"

Hank bounds up the stairs and sticks his head into the room. "Hey, Mom. Dakota, sorry

I bailed on you. I needed to feed the horses. I dropped off your stuff in your room. Is everything okay?"

I glance around the room, but I don't see my suitcases. "Where did you put my stuff?"

He jerks his head down the hall. "Your room."

"*My* room? I thought this was my room." I glance at Kat. "Our room."

"Heavens, no!" Annie Coolidge exclaims. "You have the room next to Kat's." She glares at Kat.

Kat grins at us. "I just told her she could have either bed, and I meant it. Yours to keep, if you like, Dakota."

Annie sighs. "Kat, we've been through all this. Dakota is almost 16. She needs her own room."

"Come on," Hank says. "I'll show you which one is your real room."

I follow him next door and walk into a room that's bigger than Kat's. The floors are dark wood with narrow slats, and there's a white hooked rug beside the wood bed. The white bedspread makes me think of snowflakes. Sheer white curtains hang on four long windows that open into the trees. I've never had a room to myself, and this one is something out of a book.

"I put your bags in the closet. You and Kat share the bathroom between your bedrooms. Don't be mad at Kat. She's just real glad you're here."

"I'm not mad." But I don't know what I am. I need to be alone, by myself, so I can think. "I've got a headache." It's the excuse I always use when I want to be left alone. I've been planning all along to use it as soon as I got here. Only this time it's true. I really do have a headache.

"Well," Hank says, ducking to go through the doorway, "lucky for you, there's a doctor in the house."

He starts to call his mom, but I stop him. "Please don't, Hank. I just need to lie down. I don't want to make trouble, okay? I just need to rest for a little while. Will you tell them I want to take a nap?"

I can see him thinking it over. Then he says, "Okay. Your call." He pulls the door shut as he leaves.

I hear low voices next door. Then footsteps

sound on the stairs, and I know I'm alone. I sit on the bed and feel panic seeping·in through the pores in my skin.

I try to lie down, but my whole body is twitching. There's no way I'll fall asleep. After a minute, I give up and climb out of bed. I find my backpack in the closet, drag it onto the bed, then fish out my list-book.

I have to make a list. I *need* to make a list.

I flip through pages until I come to an empty one. Then I slide to the floor, lean against the bed frame, and write:

Top 10 Reasons Why Dakota Brown
Doesn't Belong on a Nice Farm

FIVE

Top 10 Reasons Why Dakota Brown
Doesn't Belong on a Nice Farm
  1. Nice farm is too far from Nice.
  2. Nice is too far from Chicago or any
     other city.
  3. Barking dog(s).
  4. Shy, shedding cat.
  5. Who knows what's in the barn!
  6. No air-conditioning.
  7. Popeye and Annie are too over-the-top
     lovey-dovey.
  8. Computer is in the kitchen.
  9. People do chores here. Some of them outside.
  10. People on Nice farm are too nice. I'd never
     fit in.

It takes me a half hour to come up with my list, and that worries me. I've made the same kind of list in the last four foster homes, and each time I performed the task in under 10 minutes. I must be slipping.

There's a tap at my door, so soft I'm not sure I really heard it. Then it comes again.

"Come in!" I tuck my notebook into my backpack.

"You're awake!" Kat sounds way too happy. "Dad cooked fried chicken."

"Seriously?" I like fried chicken. No doubt that's what the folks ate in that *Little House on the Prairie*, too. Only no way the man of the house would have been the cook.

"And mashed potatoes and gravy," Kat adds.

I can smell it now that the door's open. Suddenly I'm starving. "Okay."

Downstairs, the others are already sitting at the table. Hank and Wes are next to each other, talking. The Coolidges sit at the head and foot of the table, so Kat and I take the two empty seats closest to the kitchen. Hank officially introduces Wes to me.

I can tell they're waiting for one of

us to say something, so I say, "I like your dog, Wes."

Wes's face transforms from street punk to choirboy. "Rex is the best." He smiles at the dog, who's lying patiently beside his chair. "He won't beg for food at the table, even when we have hamburgers."

"Yeah?" I lean so I can see the dog better. His head is between his paws, and his tail is wagging.

"Wes is a natural dog whisperer," Hank says. "He's the one who trained Rex."

I'm glad to have the dog to talk about. Otherwise, I'd have no idea what to say. "So, did you have a German shepherd before you came here?"

"Nah," he answers. "Unless you count the police dogs I used to run from."

Nobody laughs. I'm not sure if he's kidding or not.

The food's sitting on the table: chicken, mashed potatoes, broccoli, biscuits, applesauce. Plus Siamese cat salt and pepper shakers.

"Lord, what a fine meal this is!" Mr. Coolidge exclaims.

I start to say something to agree with him

when I notice that the others have their heads bowed. Then I get it. He's praying. I bow my head, but my eyes are wide open.

"You are so good to us, Father. Thank You for this food and for loving us *so* much."

Mrs. Coolidge chimes in. "And thank You for my wonderful husband, who prepared everything for us."

Back to Mr. Coolidge. "And tonight we're the most thankful to You for bringing Dakota Brown into our home. Help us to be what she needs. We know she's what we need. Amen."

Murmurs of "amen" flicker around the table. Then chairs squeak and laughter and conversation flow over everything.

I try to act normal, but I'm not sure I've ever been prayed for, and I know I've never been prayed for at dinner.

During dinner, I get the feeling Wes is watching me. I think I do okay, answering questions and making small talk. But when dinner is over, Wes carries his dishes to the kitchen, makes a turn to come up behind me, and whispers, "How long you staying?"

"What?" I ask.

He leans in so nobody else can hear.

"You're planning on taking off first chance you get, right?"

"That's crazy." I try to laugh, but he's not buying it.

"I know the signs," he says. "Don't worry. I won't be sticking around here much longer either." He calls to Kat. "Your turn to wash."

And just like that, the moment passes. But I feel more pressure than ever to make a run for it. What's to keep Wes from telling them what he knows?

Hank comes back to clear the table. "Soon as they're out of the kitchen, I can show you how to get online, if you want. Dad said you were asking about the computer."

"Great," I answer, trying not to sound too anxious. But I *am* anxious. Neil is my best hope of running away. He'll be waiting for my e-mail.

✵ ✵ ✵

It takes an hour to clean up after dinner. There's no dishwasher, so I grab a towel and help Wes dry.

"They're the only white people in the state

49

who don't have a real dishwasher," Wes complains, loud enough for the Coolidges to hear. They're bustling around the kitchen, still putting away food and cleaning counters. "Popeye refuses to get a dishwasher because he calls this 'quality family time.'"

"Popeye?" I repeat. I've been calling Mr. Coolidge "Popeye" in my head since the first time I met him. But I'd never say it to his face.

"Isn't that cute?" Annie Coolidge says, hugging her husband from behind while he struggles to put two bowls into the open fridge. "Wes has always called Chester 'Popeye.'"

"What about you, Dakota?" Mr. Coolidge asks. "You can't go on calling me 'Mr. Coolidge.' How does Popeye sound?"

This is too weird. "I don't know."

"Or 'Dad,'" Kat offers. She sets the last bowl in the drying rack.

"Popeye works," I say quickly.

Nobody's clearing out of the kitchen, so I walk outside and sit on the edge of the porch. The sun's down, but night hasn't taken over yet. A breeze carries the scent of flowers and grass.

Hank comes out and sits beside me. For a minute, neither of us says anything. Then he motions toward the barn. "Tomorrow I'll show you the horses."

I don't say anything. The only horses I've been around were plastic toys in one of the homes or pictures in books.

"Must be tough to land here for the first time," Hank says.

I shrug. "I've moved around a lot."

"Do you remember much about your family?"

Without thinking, I rattle off the story I tell everybody. "My brother was a lot older than me. He joined the army to help support the family. When he got killed, my mother couldn't take it. She died that same year, when I was five. Dad stuck it out until I was nine, but he never got over losing my mother."

"I'm sorry, Dakota," Hank says.

I ache inside, almost as if what I've just recounted is true. I've told the story so often, it feels like the truth. I can't really remember my brother, but he was killed in a gang fight. My mom had already run away by then because my dad beat her. I don't remember her at all. I was nine when my dad died of a liver disease you get from drinking too much.

"Could we check the computer now?" I ask.

"Sure." Hank gets up, and I follow him in. The only light comes from the kitchen. Upstairs, voices and footsteps filter down to us as whispers and creaks.

Hank moves the mouse, and the computer screen lights up and goes straight into e-mail. "This is Mom's account, but e-mails from the Pet Helpline come here."

He scrolls down to one from Winnie the Horse Gentler. "Great! She got back already." Hank grins at me. "Mind if I read this one before we get you going?"

"Go ahead." I scoot my chair so I can see what this Winnie person wrote.

Hey, Hank!

Tell Starlight that Nickers says hi.

Hank glances at me. "Nickers is her horse. Starlight is mine." He goes back to the screen:

52

Sorry you're still having trouble with Lancelot. From what you've told me, though, I think it's Lance's owner who has the problem, don't you? Tell her to quit looking directly into the gelding's eyes when she wants to catch him. Don't let her walk up directly from the front or from behind. Tell her to approach from the side. Then Lancelot will see her coming and won't be so surprised. That horse sounds smart to me, Hank. There's a good reason he doesn't want his owner to catch him.

Say hi to everybody for me. Catman says, "Peace."

Winnie

"She nailed it." Hank leans back in the computer chair. "She always does. I've read so many books on training horses, but Winnie just knows this stuff."

He gets up and turns the computer over to me. "I'll be out in the barn if you need me."

I wait until he leaves, then I go to my e-mail account. As I click my way through pop-up ads and junk offers, my heart starts pounding. Neil said he'd write. He said he'd be working on a way to get me out of here. Neil already has his driver's license. In another year he'll be out of the holding tank home, but he doesn't want to wait that long. Ever since we've known each other, we've talked about running away to LA.

But that's just the way Neil is. Chances are, he might forget all about me and make plans with other people. People are drawn to Neil.

I scan through spam claiming to help me lose 50 pounds in 10 days, invest my finances, vote for some politician, enhance my body parts.

Then I see it. Neil has sent me an e-mail. And the subject line reads: *California, here we come!*

MY HANDS ARE SHAKING as I click on Neil's message. I check over my shoulder to make sure nobody's watching. Then I read:

Good news, Dakota! We've got a way out to California and a job once we get there. Remember DJ from LA? He'll fix us up. And it gets better. He's coming to Chicago for some reunion thing. So you better get on it right now and work out a way to get up here. We're leaving the Fourth of July. Then we're home free!

Neil

P.S. What's it like down on the farm? Ha!

My first reaction is to jump up from the computer chair and scream, "California, here I come!" I jump up, but I don't scream. And I sit back down. DJ isn't a guy I'd choose to travel with. I only met him once, and he gave me the creeps. But if he can get me to California, then he's okay by me.

I reread Neil's e-mail. Then I hit Reply.

Neil, cool! Count me in, and tell DJ to save me a seat to California. One small detail—how am I supposed to get up to Chicago on the Fourth?

☆ ☆ ☆

The next morning, I wake up to the sound of rushing water. I jump out of bed and glance wildly around the room. It takes me a second to remember where I am and to figure out that the rushing water is only a toilet flushing, the one I share with Kat.

I grab the blanket off my bed and wrap it around my shoulders. Then I close the windows and wait until I hear Kat leave the bathroom. But when I open my door to the john, her door springs back open.

"You're up!" Kat sticks her head in, and it's all I can do not to gasp. The red hair is gone. In its place is long, straight black hair down to her waist.

"Your hair?" I say stupidly.

"Like it?" she asks, doing that angel smile of hers. She rubs her cheek against the kitten she's holding.

"It's different," I say, trying to decide if *this* is the real Kat.

"Thanks! I like different."

"Me too." I reach out to pet her kitten, but it squirms to get away.

"Don't take it personally," Kat says. "Kitten's shy. I'm going to write Catman about her." She runs her finger along the kitten's gray-white head. "Better hurry. You missed Mom, but Dad made breakfast." She dips out, closing the door after her.

"Morning, Dakota!" Popeye calls when I come downstairs.

"Morning . . . Popeye," I answer, trying the name out loud. He doesn't flinch.

"Sad, sad, sad that you missed Miami. She looked radiant today. I tell you, that woman gets more beautiful every day! Don't you agree, Wes?"

"Whatever." Wes is working through a stack of pancakes that appear to be dog shaped. Rex is at his feet.

I pour myself a glass of juice. Dogs are barking somewhere. "Is that coming from upstairs?"

"Yeah." Wes says this like I've challenged him to a duel. "So?"

Popeye smiles at both of us. "You'll have to get Wes to tell you about his dog business. He's placed over two dozen dogs, and none have been returned."

"Cool. Mind if I check e-mail?" I ask.

"Be my guest." Popeye stabs a bacon strip and slaps it into the frying pan. "Never quite took to the e-mail. Give me *real* junk mail, the kind that shows up in the mailbox out front. And love letters! What would have become of all my love letters to Miami if they'd been love e-mails? Which reminds me . . ." He grabs a handful of letters from the counter and hands them to Wes. "Wes, would you run these out to the mailbox and put the flag up so the postman will take them? He'll be here any minute."

Wes sighs, but he does it.

I move to the computer. When the screen pops on, I'm in someone's in-box. "Okay if I close out of this account and go to mine?"

"Go right ahead," Popeye says, still frying up bacon. "Miami forgets when she's in a hurry, which she always is. Now, she's a different story when it comes to e-mail. Uses it all the time. Why, I remember one time when . . ."

I'm only half listening as I log in to my account.

Yes! Neil's written me back already. Right below my question "How am I supposed to get up to Chicago?" Neil's written one word: *Drive.*

This is so Neil. Just because he never worries about anything and always finds a way to get what he wants, he thinks everybody should be like that. I check when he sent the e-mail. Three minutes ago. I don't see instant messenger on this computer, but there's a chance I can catch Neil while he's still online.

As fast as I can, I type a reply:

Neil, how am I going to drive to Chicago?

A. I don't have a car.

B. I don't know how to drive!

59

I hit Send and wait.

"Dakota, would you like a short stack of pancakes?" Popeye asks.

"No thanks," I answer, staring at the screen, willing an e-mail to appear.

"We must eat to keep up our strength," Popeye insists.

"Okay."

Ding. New mail.

It's from Neil. He's actually there, at the other end of cyberspace. Neil has typed in answers to my twofold question:

Dakota says: I don't have a car.

Neil says: GET ONE.

Dakota says: I don't know how to drive.

Neil says: LEARN.

Thanks a lot, Neil.

I log off, knowing that's as far as I can take this with Neil. What he's saying between the lines is: *Dakota, grow up. If I can get you from Chicago to California, the least you can do is get to Chicago.*

And he's right. It's up to me.

As soon as I sit at the table, Popeye sets down a plate of horse-head pancakes. "Would you prefer cats or dogs?" he offers.

"Horses are good," I assure him.

Wes comes back from the mailbox, snaps a leash on Rex, and leaves without a word. This kid really doesn't like me.

Kat walks through the kitchen, carrying four cats and tossing me a smile before going outside.

I wolf down the pancakes, which turn out to be pretty good as long as I don't think of it as biting off a horse's ear. Then I head outside, glad for the alone time. I need to work things out. How am I going to learn to drive, and what can I drive to Chicago?

As I walk toward the barn, I gaze up at the blue sky streaked with wisps of white.

"Heads up!"

I turn in time to see Hank riding a big, brown horse straight at me.

"Dakota! Out of the way!" he shouts.

I scurry backwards as horse and Hank race by me in a blur. A few yards up the hill, the horse stops. It trots in small circles for a while before settling to a prancing walk.

My heart is still pounding at the close call, but I can't take my gaze off the beautiful horse with a black mane that flows over its arched neck. It looks like the pictures I used to cut out of horse magazines and get in trouble for when the library reported on me. I think it's a bay, but what I know about horses only comes from books.

When I was kid, I went through a horse-crazy stage, which was pretty stupid since I'd never even touched a real horse. I used to beg my dad for a horse. He'd laugh. Then I begged him to take me somewhere so I could at least see a real horse. He'd raise his arm and pull it back, like he was going to hit me. I don't have a single photo of my parents, but that's the picture of Dad I carry around in my head: one arm raised, ready to hit, the other hand wrapped around a beer can.

After Dad died and I went to live with the first foster family, I checked out horse books from the library and read every horse story I could find. I stopped when I realized I'd never own a horse of my own, no matter what I did.

Hank rides up to me, but I can tell he's in control now. He's riding English—no saddle horn, and a four-rein bridle. "Dakota, I'm sorry. He just got away from me. You okay?"

"I'm okay," I answer, breathing in the smell of horse. It's sweet and powerful. This is the closest I've ever been to a horse. I want to touch him so much.

Hank reaches down and strokes the horse's sweaty neck. The bay relaxes, but his eyes flick, like he's watching for the enemy.

Hank keeps scratching under the bay's mane.

The scratching stops, and Hank grins sheepishly at me. "I'm really sorry about that. I'm trying to work the kinks out of this fella so his owners won't trade him in. He's a good horse. He's just never been handled right. I can't believe they've been riding him with this bit. It's a bad fit. He caught it between his teeth, held on, and that was that. I couldn't control him. I'm switching to a snaffle."

"With the break in the middle?" I ask, picturing a page of bits from one of the library books I memorized when I was a kid.

Hank looks surprised, but he doesn't ask.

"That's the one." He leans forward and smooths the bay's mane.

"He's beautiful." I reach to pet him, but he tosses his head.

"Come on, Lancelot," Hank coos. "You're such a good boy. You've just got more than your share of bad habits. Not your fault." Hank smiles at me. His mouth is crooked, in kind of a cute way. "This is the horse I wrote Winnie about yesterday."

"Maybe you better write her again," I suggest, wondering if he'll get the tease.

He gets it. I can tell by his crooked grin. "You want to meet a truly great horse? Meet me in the barn." He starts off on Lancelot, then pivots around. "Give me 15 minutes to cool this one down. Then I'll introduce you to Starlight. She's worth the wait."

"Starlight?" I repeat. "As in Starlight Animal Rescue?"

"Yep!" he calls back. "Don't go anywhere."

This reminds me that I need very much to go somewhere. Chicago. Why am I fooling with horses when what I really need is a car?

Annie Coolidge's red sports car is out of the question. She probably drives it to work every day. I'd be afraid to borrow it anyway. I need something older. When I get to Chicago, I'll let them know where they can pick it up. I'm not a car thief.

There's not another car in sight on the property. Still, I can't imagine they'd be stuck out here without one. With his duties as a part-time fireman, Popeye's got to have wheels.

I decide to explore. I circle the house, but there's nothing. Then I lap the barn. Parked at the far end is an old beater pickup, with a snub nose, rusted high fenders, a metal truck bed, and a missing tailgate. I'm guessing this monstrosity has got to be 50 years old. Could it still run?

I walk closer. The tires are good. I glance both ways, then get in. The seat's huge, with gray tape stuck at weird angles to hold in the foam stuffing. It smells like hay and manure. My feet don't reach the pedals.

I go for the glove compartment and bump into the knobbed stick on the floor. Great. So not only do I have to learn to drive, I have to learn to drive a stick shift.

I feel around the glove box for a key. Nothing. I check the visor. It's there. At least

I can find out if the old truck will start. I stick the key in the ignition and turn when someone yells:

"Hey! What are you doing in there?"

SEVEN

"YOU HEARD ME! What do you think you're doing?"

I nearly jump out of my skin at the shrill voice.

A girl about my age is standing at the window, glaring in at me. "This is private property." She narrows green eyes at me. Her auburn hair is short and stylish. I'm not sure what her face looks like because she's wearing enough makeup to put on her own theater production. Her name-brand jeans cost more than everything in my suitcase. "Well? What are you doing in Hank's truck?"

So the truck is Hank's? I don't answer her. I open the truck door, and she has to step back or be hit by it. Neil taught me that the best defense is a good offense. I shift into my best *offensive* manner. "*I* live here. This is *my* home. And the last time I looked, you weren't part of it. *You're* the one on private property."

"*Me?*" she asks, sounding outraged. "Hank and I are . . . friends! I've never seen you around here before. Who are you?"

"Who are *you?*" I ask, not backing off. "What are you doing here?"

"My horse is here! Hank is helping me train it."

"Lancelot, right?" That makes sense. No wonder the poor horse is so mixed up.

She nods. I think I've surprised her again by knowing her horse's name.

"So," I say, taking a step toward her, "what's your name?"

"Guinevere."

I laugh. "Cute. What's your real name?"

Her eyes get even skinnier—green slits under perfectly plucked eyebrows. "Guinevere!"

"Oh." I think she's telling the truth. Maybe it's time to make nice and play well with others. "So, what do they call you? Gwen? Gwenie?"

"Guinevere," she says through clenched teeth.

Hank strolls out from the barn. "Hey! I didn't hear you drive up."

Guinevere doesn't turn from our stare-down. "I didn't. Daddy dropped me off at the road, and I walked in. Then I found *her* in your truck."

"Great!" Hank says, sounding totally clueless to the drama before him. "Then you two met already?"

"Gwen and I are gal pals," I answer. "Could I meet Starlight now?"

"Sure." Hank turns back to the barn, and Guinevere shoves me aside to walk next to him.

"Who *is* she?" Guinevere whispers.

"I'm sorry," Hank says, turning back to me. "I thought you guys did this already. Dakota, this is Guinevere La Roche. Guinevere, Dakota Brown."

"Dakota?" Now it's her turn to laugh. "And you made fun of *my* name? What kind of a name is 'Dakota' anyway?"

On cue, I let my face fall. I stare at my

fingers and let my voice shake. "It's . . . it's the only name I have. My parents abandoned me on the plains of North Dakota when I was just a baby. I was almost dead when Indians found me. They called me 'Dakota' because that's all they knew about me. The foster system added 'Brown.'"

It isn't true. None of it. But the story gets the reaction it always does.

"Oh wow," Guinevere says, her mouth curling as if she's eaten something sour.

Hank's crooked grin half forms on his lips. I can almost see his brain connecting the dots. "Right. So, you want to see Starlight or not?"

In answer, I stride ahead of them and into the barn. It takes a second for my eyes to adjust from the bright sunshine, but there's quite a bit of light inside the barn too. Windows let in sunshine all along the loft. I can see four stalls, and there are probably four more on the other aisle. The front half of the barn is taken up by a wooden, circular pen.

Lancelot stands at the far end of the pen. But when he hears us, he starts walking over. Then he sees Guinevere. His ears flatten, and he stops in the center of the ring.

"Hank," Guinevere whines, "you said you'd teach him to come to me."

"I'm working on it," Hank says, climbing into the pen with Lancelot.

I want to see how he handles the horse, so I climb in too.

Guinevere glances from Hank to me like she'd better not get left out. Then she climbs in. "Here, Lancelot," she calls, striding toward the horse.

"Don't walk straight at him," Hank cautions.

"What?" Even as she says it, it's clear that she heard Hank. She just doesn't like being told what to do.

"Come at him from the side," Hank says. "That way he'll see you coming and won't be so scared of you."

"Scared of *me*? My horse is probably scared of *her*." Guinevere points in my direction. She takes a few steps toward her horse, and he trots away.

"I've just about had it with that horse," she complains. "Maybe Daddy's right and I just picked the wrong horse. Daddy found this beautiful five-gaited mare in Indiana."

"Don't give up on Lance," Hank begs. "I just need more time with him."

She smiles at Hank, softens, and becomes a sweet, flirty Guinevere I haven't seen before. Truth is, I don't like this Guinevere any better than the other Guineveres I've seen today. "Well, I guess more time with Lancelot means more time with me."

I think I may puke. Since I haven't budged from my spot by the railing, I start to climb out the way I came in.

"Wait, Dakota," Hank calls. "Where are you going?"

"To find Starlight," I answer.

"I'll come with you," he says, jogging to the fence and bounding over it. "Starlight's over this way."

I follow and wait for him to open the stall door. The top half of the double door is already open. Before he steps inside, he's greeted by a gorgeous brown and white Paint.

"Starlight," Hank says, scratching the mare under her chin until she stretches her neck toward him in pure pleasure, "this is Dakota."

"She's great." I step around for a better look. "How long–?" I stop. I can see now that

72

something's wrong with her eyes. Really wrong. They're white and shiny, like solid marbles. "Hank, what happened to your horse?" My voice cracks on "horse," and something catches in my throat.

"She's okay, Dakota. I'm sorry. I should have warned you. I forget what it looks like to other people. Starlight was born blind. Her owner wanted to put her down. The vet told Dad, and we brought her home with us. The dam, her mother, died giving birth to her, so we had to feed her from a bottle. We almost lost her. She was our first animal rescue."

"So you named the place after her. And she gets along okay?" I realize that I'm stroking her neck the way Hank had stroked Lancelot's neck. She's soft and warm, and she doesn't flinch or try to get away from me.

"Better than okay." Hank pulls a metal hook from his back pocket and starts cleaning her hooves. "It was tough for a long time, even after we knew she'd live. She was scared of everything because she couldn't see what was coming at her."

"And now?"

"Now she's spook-proof. I can ride her

in a parade and she won't shy." Hank cleans her back hooves, then returns to her head. "I couldn't ask for a better horse."

"Hank!" Guinevere shouts from the pen. I can only imagine how her horse hates that shrill shout.

Hank grins at me. "Better go."

"Are you doing this as a favor to Guinevere?" I ask, wondering how he could stand to have her around.

"Kind of. Partly for the fee her dad pays. We use it to run the Rescue. I guess I'm mostly doing it for Lancelot, though. I'm afraid they'll sell him at auction, and who knows where he'll end up? The Rescue is his last chance."

"Hank!" Guinevere's shout has turned to a whine.

Hank leaves the stall, letting me stay where I am. I can't believe he's not afraid I'll hurt his horse. I stay with the mare for quite a while, hoping Guinevere will be gone when I come out.

No such luck. When I walk up the barn aisle, I see her hanging all over Hank while he tries to explain something about Lancelot. I slip around to the other aisle, out of sight, and tiptoe past the stalls.

When I get to the end, I hear Guinevere's laugh. It sounds like she's coming toward me. I duck into the nearest stall.

"She's probably gone back to the house, Hank," Guinevere says. "I can't believe your parents would take on another foster kid, especially one who's so old."

"It'll be fine," Hank says.

"Fine, then. But come on back. I don't have all day."

I hear footsteps walking away and Hank saying something I can't make out.

The stalls on this side of the barn aren't as bright as the other side. It takes my eyes a second to adjust. When I glance behind me, I see a dark shadow. My hand flies to my mouth to keep me from screaming.

It's a horse, huddled in the far corner of the stall. He's black—the blackest black I've ever seen—without a white hair on him. Black as fire, I think, although I know fire isn't black. Somehow it fits, though. I stare at him. He's taller than Starlight, but leaner. Not a quarter horse. His muscles ripple on his neck and rump. I think he's quivering. He's scared.

"Hey, Blackfire," I whisper. "It's only me. I'm a lot more scared than you are."

The horse doesn't move, and neither do I. But I can't stop staring at him. Then he cranes his neck around and looks right at me. Maybe right through me. Popeye's words come back to me, the way he said he could feel the wood-pecker's tapping in his soul. That's where I feel the beauty of this horse.

I don't know how long we stand like that. Finally Blackfire lifts his hoof and sets it down in my direction. Then the other hoof. And little by little, he makes his way across the stall until he's inches from me.

I don't move, but it has nothing to do with fear. I don't want him to go away. His ears flick back and forth, but they don't go flat back like Lancelot's did.

He stretches out his neck until his nose, his muzzle, brushes against my arm. I shiver inside. It feels like velvet. His nostrils go in and out, getting big, then smaller, as he takes in my scent. I drink in his scent too. He nuzzles me, moving his muzzle along my arm, up my shoulder to my head.

I remember reading once that horses use

their noses as fingers, touching their world and checking it out. I think we should all have muzzles. I close my eyes as he nuzzles my face and shares his warm breath.

I blow back, right into his nostrils. He returns the favor. I reach out slowly and touch his neck. It's soft and smooth. I move my hand up his neck until I reach his jaw. As I scratch his jaw, he sticks out his chin and closes his eyes to half-mast. If there's a heaven, it must be like this.

"Now where are you going?" Guinevere's sharp voice startles both of us.

Blackfire retreats to the back of the stall.

I duck out of the stall and close the latch.

"Dakota?" Hank strides up the aisle toward me. "I thought you went back to the house."

I shrug. "I'm just looking around. That's okay, isn't it?" I ask, taking on the role of the poor orphan waif, eager to please.

"Of course," Hank answers. "Just don't get too close to this horse."

"Why?"

"He was pretty badly abused before his owner got him. Actually, my grandmother bought him because she'd seen him mistreated.

I'm trying to settle him for her, but he won't let me near him."

"Your grandmother rides horses?" I ask.

Hank laughs. "You obviously haven't met Gram. She loves all animals, from a respectable distance."

Guinevere scurries up to stand between us. "They didn't call that horse 'Black Devil' for nothing. I've been telling Hank he shouldn't waste his time. He can't save every horse on the planet."

"He doesn't look wild to me," I say, afraid to tell them I've been petting his grandmother's horse.

"That's because you're not in there with him," Guinevere says. She leans into Hank. "Let's go back and work with Lancelot, Hank. I want to ride."

Hank takes one more look at Blackfire. I will never call him Black Devil. They're so wrong about this horse. Then Hank lets himself be pulled away by the impatient Lady Guinevere.

He glances back over his shoulder as she pulls him up the aisle. "You can watch if you want, Dakota."

But I'm already heading out of the barn. "Thanks. I'm good. I've got stuff to do inside."

What I do inside is take out my list-book and start a new page:

TOP 10 REASONS NOT TO LIKE GUINEVERE
1. The stuck-up name fits.
2. She's Cruella De Vil . . . without the heart.
3. She's Frankenstein . . . without Frank's charm.
4. She's Cinderella's stepmother . . . without the sense of fair play.
5. She's the Joker . . . without his sense of humor.
6. She's Lex Luthor . . . without the goodwill.
7. She's Montana Max and Yosemite Sam rolled into one . . . without their sweetness.
8. She's Sheldon J. Plankton . . . without the good taste.
9. She's Dracula . . . without his unselfishness.
10. She's Captain Hook . . . without the kindness.

EIGHT

WEDNESDAY I SLEEP IN ON PURPOSE. Then I lie in bed another hour, reliving my time with Blackfire. It feels so much like a dream that I'm almost afraid to go back to the barn.

When I finally venture out of my room, Kat is sitting on the top step, blocking the stairs. She's holding her kitten, plus two bigger cats. She grins at me and whispers, "Barney and Fred don't like each other. I'm trying to find them separate owners."

"Did somebody dump the cats here?" I wonder how often this happens and if they can possibly find homes for all the animals. But it's not my problem.

Kat shakes her head. Her hair is working itself out of the still-black ponytail it's stuck in. So I figure black must be her real color.

"We got Fred on his last day at the animal shelter. Barney belonged to one of Gram's friends who died. We'll find him a good home. He's a great cat."

"Hank's grandmother is the one who brought over that black horse in the barn, right?" I'm trying to imagine an old lady who saves animals but doesn't like them.

"Yeah. Did you see that horse? He's really wild."

"So they say." I ease by her on the steps. Fred squirms and tries to get loose, but Barney doesn't budge. Kat's kitten hides its head under her arm. "Do you know where Hank is?"

"I think he went for a ride on Starlight. Mom's at the hospital, of course. Dad's in town getting groceries."

Cool! Blackfire should be by himself. I rush downstairs and outside. The screen door slams behind me, and I hear dogs barking. Two smallish mutts race across the yard toward me, yapping like crazy. I don't know whether to wait and see if they're all bark and no bite or try to make it back to the house.

But before I can decide, they're on me. The gray, long-haired mutt growls and grabs my shoelace. I shake my foot to get him to let go, but he won't. "Let go of me!"

The other dog, a Chihuahua, yaps even louder and shows its teeth.

Wes comes running up with Rex behind him. "Stop yelling!"

"Tell the dogs to stop yelling!" I snap. "Get them off of me, Wes!"

Wes glances over his shoulder, and now I see there's a big white car that's pulled up. An older woman in a straw hat is standing by the car.

"You're ruining everything!" Wes snarls at me. "Go back inside."

"That's what I was trying to do when your attack dogs attacked." I step around Wes, but I can't get away from the shoelace-chewing mutt.

Wes reaches down and grabs both dogs, tucking one under each arm. "Why did you have to come here?" He shoots me a look that would wilt roses, then carries the dogs toward the white car.

All I can think is that maybe this woman is trying to dump these two dogs. My vote on that one is *no*. So I follow Wes.

"Sorry about that, ma'am," Wes says, as if he's this perfect gentleman. He walks up to the woman, who has one hand on the car door handle. "Do you want to hold one of them? See how soft he is?"

"I don't think so," the woman says. A smile flickers on her lips, then fades.

"But you were saying you thought Taco might be perfect for you. He won't shed. He could go on vacations with you." Wes holds out the Chihuahua, but the woman backs away.

"No," she says. "I don't think either dog suits."

Then I get it. Wes has been trying to place one of the dogs with this woman. Not the other way around.

"But . . ." Wes moves closer.

The woman opens the driver's door and gets in. Her hat scrapes the car roof and almost falls off. "I can't have a barking dog in the condo. Or one that might attack my neighbors."

"They don't attack people!" Wes insists. "And they almost never bark." He glares over his shoulder at me.

"Thank you anyway, young man." She closes the door and gives a little wave from behind her closed window. Then she starts the car and drives off.

Wes turns to me. "Thanks a lot!" His glare is filled with hate. If he didn't have a dog in each arm, I'm not sure what he'd do. "You just wrecked two weeks of work. She would have taken this dog if it hadn't been for you."

"And she probably would have brought it back when it attacked one of her neighbors!" I shout back, taking the offensive, even though I feel pretty lousy about denying the dog a good home. What if it never gets a home? What then? I shove that thought out of my head and glare at Wes.

"Why did you have to come here?" Wes mutters. He shakes his head and walks past me to the house.

I want to shout after him: *I didn't choose to be here! And I'm leaving as soon as I can!* But I don't.

I wait until I hear Wes talking to Kat on

the stairs. Then I run to the barn. I want to see Blackfire. It's stupid. I know that. But I *need* to see him.

The minute I open Blackfire's stall door, he makes a low, soft horse sound. I think it's called a nicker, and it's instantly my favorite sound in the whole world. I want to bottle his nicker and carry it with me to California.

"Hey, boy." I remember exactly where he liked being scratched, so I do it again. "You're a good boy, aren't you? I'm sorry somebody was mean to you and gave you that awful name."

He nuzzles my neck while I keep scratching. "You're Blackfire now." I think looking at, and feeling, this horse is the biggest proof I've ever had that there's a God. Blackfire couldn't have been an accident. He had to be created by *Somebody*.

Outside, the wind kicks up. A branch scratches at the loft window above the stall. Blackfire jerks away.

"It's okay." I walk to him and stroke his beautiful head. His eyes are as black as the rest of him, intelligent, not missing a thing. I want to help Blackfire before I leave with Neil. But I have no idea how to go about it. I could ask

Hank, but I'm afraid he might tell me I can't hang out with the horse.

Then I remember the e-mail girl Hank writes when he has a question about horses. *Winnie the Horse Gentler!* Why not ask her? She wouldn't even have to know who I am. All I'd have to do is write her at that Pet Helpline.

I stay with Blackfire all afternoon, until I hear Popeye drive up in the truck. Then I help him carry in groceries. At least half of the bags are filled with cat food and dog food.

Kat comes out to help, and I do a double take when I see her hair. She's wearing long, blonde braids that look the most like the real Kat.

"I like your hair," I say, plopping a bag of dog treats on the kitchen counter.

"Me too," she says. "I like yours."

Together, we put away groceries while Popeye goes looking for Wes.

"Kat," I ask when I'm sure we're alone, "will you show me how you e-mail Catman?"

"Sure," she answers, climbing up on the counter to put the brown sugar on a top shelf. "But if it's about cats, I might know the answer."

"I'm sure you would. I want to write Winnie, though. I've got a couple of horse questions."

"Why don't you ask Hank? He knows everything about horses." She hops down from the counter, and I think I see her wince.

"You okay?" I ask.

"Yeah." But she looks even paler than usual. She takes a seat at the table. I think she may have hurt herself when she jumped.

"Sit tight," I command. "I've got the rest of the groceries."

She doesn't argue.

"Don't say anything to Hank about me writing Winnie, okay?" I search cupboards until I find the spot for cereal boxes.

She tilts her head. "He wouldn't care. You can trust Hank, Dakota. We're family now."

I stop taking cans out of the plastic bag and turn to her. "*You're* family, Kat." I stop before I say something that might hurt her feelings. "I haven't had family since I was nine." And even then, it wasn't what Kat's thinking of when she talks about family.

"Want to know what my favorite verse in the Bible is?" she asks, picking up her kitten, who's sneaked in from somewhere. Kat doesn't wait for me to answer. "'See how very much our Father loves us, for he calls us his children, and that is what we are!'"

Something inside of me hurts. I can tell Kat feels that love, the love of a father. She has a peace about her you can almost feel yourself. I can't even imagine what that would be like. I'm not sure I've ever felt the love of a father.

I put on my game face and grin at her. "Not a bad deal for you, Kat. Must make life pretty easy having God as your dad."

She smiles back at me. "It helps a lot." She stands, and I see her steady herself with one hand on the table before she speaks. I can't help thinking something's wrong with her. "Want to e-mail Winnie now?"

"If you're sure you're okay."

She flashes me that full-court smile and sits at the computer, and I think I must be imagining things. In minutes we're logged on to Annie Coolidge's e-mail account, and Kat has found the e-mail address in Annie's contact list. "The only person I e-mail is Catman, so I didn't bother opening another e-mail account.

Mom lets me use hers." She clicks in Winnie's e-mail address and gets up. "All set."

"Thanks, Kat."

It feels funny writing someone I don't even know.

Dear Winnie,

I admit I don't have much experience with horses. I've never taken a riding lesson or horsemanship class. To be honest, yesterday was the first time I actually touched a horse. But I'm staying where there's this abused horse that, for some crazy reason, seems to like me. He lets me pet him and scratch his jaw.

What I need to know is where to go from here. How can I help this horse? I don't have much time, so the sooner you can give me an answer, the better.

Thanks,

Don't-know-much-about-horses

Before I lose my nerve, I hit Send.

NINE

I FINISH PUTTING AWAY GROCERIES. Then I get an apple out of the fridge and pour myself a glass of milk. I'm halfway through the apple when I hear the *ding* that means new e-mail has arrived. I know it couldn't possibly be Winnie already, but I check just in case. And it is!

Dear Horsewoman,

Yep, I know you don't think of yourself as one. But you are! It says a lot that the abused horse chose you. He sensed something good in you, someone he can trust. Horsemanship is more than knowing how to post in a saddle or win a blue ribbon. It's communicating with your horse. So you're off to an amazing start!

Since you haven't been around horses, you need to observe them. Watch how they relate to each other. I admit that I recognized this e-mail address right away, even though I don't know who you are exactly. But I won't tell Hank or anybody there that we're e-mailing. That's your call, okay? At least I know you have horses to watch at Starlight Animal Rescue. One will be the leader, the dominant horse. The others are more content because they trust the leader. They don't mind letting a dominant mare go first. They'll gladly move over if she wants their spot. They respect her.

That's the role you need with this abused horse. You need his love and respect. Then he'll do what you ask.

So how do you become the leader? Not with force. Your horse would win that one. Plus, somebody already tried force with your horse. Instead, ask. Ask your horse to do what you want him to do. If you want him to move over, touch his side with your finger. Don't keep pushing. Touch, then release. If he doesn't move, touch again with a little more pressure. Then release. And do it again. And again—until he's so annoyed with you, he moves. Don't force, but don't stop until you get the behavior you want.

That's enough for today. But I'll be here. Write me again!

Winnie

I'm so excited. I want to write back and thank her. But Wes and Popeye come in, then Hank and Kat. And we all fall into dinner preparations—slicing celery, making salad, filling water glasses, and setting the table, while Popeye works his magic with the fish he brought home from the market. Wes keeps as far away from me as possible.

Just as Popeye turns the skillet to warm, I hear a car drive up. "Miami!" Popeye cries. He drops the fryer spatula and runs outside.

Hank takes over cooking the fish. "Something tells me Mom's home."

From the kitchen, I hear Popeye greet his wife as if they haven't seen each other in years.

"Are they for real?" I ask Hank.

"Real as it gets, Dakota," he answers.

Popeye rearranges seating at the table so he can sit next to his wife tonight. He prays for the food and for each one of us and for a lot of things—the smell of fresh-cut hay, Kat's new hairdo, Rex the dog, and finally the fish.

Annie asks how our days went, and she starts with me.

"Fine," I reply.

Wes harrumphs.

I go on as if I haven't heard him. "I hung out in the barn. And I almost got eaten by a pack of wild dogs."

"She wrecked a pet adoption!" Wes shouts.

"Wes, lower your voice, please," Popeye says.

"I'm sure there's more to this story, Wes," Annie says, passing him the salad. He doesn't take it. "Tell us what happened, honey."

"No." He stares at his plate in heavy silence.

"All right," Annie says calmly. "Let us know if you change your mind. Kat, what did you do today?"

Kat tells us about Kitten's new hiding place

in the barn. "And I got a promising application for Barney the cat."

"Application?" I ask.

"That's one way we place abandoned pets," Kat explains. "We won't let them go with just anybody."

Hank reports on Lancelot's progress, or lack of it.

Then Annie turns to her husband. They're sitting so close together that their noses touch. "Any progress on the latest rhyming book?"

I nudge Kat and whisper, "Rhyming book?"

She whispers back, "Dad writes children's books."

"You're kidding," I say, louder than I meant to.

Popeye balances his knife and fork across his plate and rubs his hands together. "Two promising projects," he says, like he's giving away a secret. "One is about a unicorn, or maybe a camel, who doesn't want to go on Noah's ark. So the poor creature says, 'Can't you see it's way too scary? Is this whole trip necessary?'"

"Brilliant!" Annie exclaims. She kisses Popeye's bald head.

"Nice rhyme, Dad," Hank adds, grinning at me.

"I think you should make it a cat instead of a unicorn," Kat suggests.

"Wonderful idea, Kat!" Popeye exclaims.

"What's the other story about?" Annie asks, taking a bite of her fish.

"Thought you'd never ask," Popeye jokes. "Mice. Not sure where this one is going, but I do like the sound of the words."

"Hit it, Dad," Hank says.

Popeye clears his throat and recites the lines as if he's in an elementary school recital: "Do Mice Sneeze?" He clears his throat again. "Do mice sneeze? When they sneeze, do they buckle at their little mice knees? Do their ears blow free in the wintry breeze? Do they scuse themselves, saying, 'Scuse me, please'?" He glances around the table for approval. "There's more, but that's enough for now."

"Marvelous!" His wife kisses his head again.

Popeye's face reddens. "Well, it has a nice sound. But like I said, I don't know where it's headed. There's more plot on a cereal box than in the mice story."

"I like it, Dad," Kat says. "Bet you could work a cat into that one, too."

"I'll bet I could," Popeye agrees.

I'm wondering if he's actually sold one of these rhyming books, but I don't ask.

Conversations break off as we work through dinner. Kat just picks at her food.

Suddenly, she stands up from the table. "I need to be excused."

The smiles vanish from every face. "Want me to come?" Annie asks.

Kat shakes her head and runs up the stairs.

It's so quiet I can hear a woodpecker tapping outside. "She hopped down from the counter earlier, and I thought maybe she hurt herself."

"No," Popeye says. "I doubt it."

We eat in silence for a couple of minutes. Then Popeye smiles and says, "Talked to Ms. Bean today. She and her honey want to meet us in Nice for fireworks on the Fourth."

"They can meet us at the Made-Rite," Annie agrees.

I've been waiting the whole meal to ask my big question. Now's as good a time as any. "I was wondering . . . ," I begin.

"What's that?" Annie asks, pushing away her plate.

"I'm almost 16—"

Hank interrupts. "Which is why we're celebrating both of our birthdays at the Made-Rite."

I smile at him, then turn to Popeye. "I want to learn how to drive. I know Hank drives, right? Guinevere said the truck is his."

"Will be," Popeye corrects, "when Hank turns 16 and passes the driving test. He's a first-rate driver already, though."

"Dad has let me drive the truck around the farm since I was Wes's age. Comes in handy around here. Can't wait to get my license, though. I'm taking the test right after my birthday."

I turn to Annie and Popeye. "Would you ever have time to teach me how to drive?"

"Sure!" they both answer at the same time.

"Sure?" Wes says. He throws his napkin onto his plate. "Sure? She just got here! I've been here a year, and nobody's bothered to teach me to drive."

"You're only 14," Popeye reminds him.

"Hank just said he was driving at my age."

"Lower your voice, Wes," Annie says. "Look at it this way. If Dakota gets her license, maybe she'll teach you to drive."

"No thanks! I don't want anything from her!" He spits out the words.

"Wes!" Popeye says. "What's gotten into you?"

Wes shoots me a look to injure. "I would have placed Taco with Mrs. O'Malley if it hadn't been for *her*."

I start to defend myself, but Annie takes over. "Wes, calm down. Dakota's part of this family too, and—"

Wes gets up so fast his chair tips over backwards. Rex explodes in a fit of barking. "Family? *She's* not my family! And you're not my mother! I'm writing *my* mom and telling her to come get me. I'm not staying here, and you can't make me!"

He storms away from the table with Rex barking at his heels. Popeye starts to go after him, but Annie puts her hand on his arm, and he sits down again.

I feel like it's my fault. "I didn't mean to wreck anything."

"Dakota, it's not your fault," Hank says.

"Of course not." Annie's voice is soft, soothing. "I don't think even Wes believes that, really. He'll come around."

I doubt it. "Do you think his mother will come and get him?"

Annie and Popeye exchange a look and seem to agree without words. Then Popeye explains, almost in a whisper. "Wes's mother has some serious problems. Wes came to live with us because she went to prison for dealing drugs. She's in rehab now, and we pray for her every night."

Annie's eyes are tearing up. "But even if she gets out of rehab and on her feet again, the courts won't let her have Wes back."

"Why?" I've always been jealous of kids who had even one parent in the picture. But I've never imagined having a parent some judge said you couldn't be with. Maybe that's worse. You'd have to be a pretty lousy mother for the courts to say you couldn't keep your own kid.

"I think that's Wes's story to tell if he ever decides he wants to tell it," Annie says. She takes a deep breath and shifts gears. "So, Dakota, back to driving lessons. When do you want to start?"

"Tonight? Tomorrow?" I'm more anxious than ever to get the plan rolling.

Annie gazes at her husband. "Looks like a job for Popeye. I'll have my car at the hospital." She smiles at me. "I've always said a gal needs to know how to drive a stick shift. Think you can learn on the truck?"

I don't have much choice. "Sure."

"Tomorrow then." Popeye gets up from the table and clears his and his wife's dishes.

"Guess I better watch where I'm riding tomorrow," Hank comments. He picks up his and Wes's plates and carries them to the kitchen.

I take the cue and clear for Kat and me.

After dinner, I read in my room until I'm sure everybody else is asleep. Then I slip downstairs and sneak outside to the barn. A moon-slice shines through the branches of the big oak and reflects off the barn roof, making the barn look like a purple shadow. I've never seen so many stars in my whole life. I think I know where they got the name "Starlight" for Hank's horse and the Rescue.

Inside the barn, I make my way to Blackfire's stall and tell him good night.

"Tomorrow I'm going to watch you," I whisper. I stay for a few minutes, then sneak back to my room.

As I lie in bed, I listen to the creaking of the farmhouse. Inside my mind, there's a ticking, like a clock running down. I have a week and a half to learn to drive.

I am running out of time.

And so is Blackfire.

TEN

I **THINK** I'm the first one up and out the door the next morning. I can't wait to start watching the horses. But when I jog to the barn, Hank's already there.

"Man, you're up early," he says.

I'm disappointed that I've missed how the horses start their day. "Did you feed them already?"

"Yeah. Starlight gets feisty if she has to wait too long. Then the others join in." He walks into Starlight's stall and unlatches the rear door that opens to the pasture.

If the others join in, then maybe Starlight's

the lead, or dominant, mare. But I want to observe the horses together so I can see for myself. "Want me to let the other horses out with Starlight?"

Hank stares after his horse as she kicks up her heels and takes off at a gallop. "I better let Lance and Black out."

At least he doesn't call the horse Black Devil. He lets Lancelot out, and the gelding takes off like Starlight did, tossing his mane and twisting his neck.

Then we move to Blackfire's stall on the other side of the barn.

Hank slips into the stall and unlatches the back door. "This puts him in the same pasture as the others. Stay there. I never know what he'll do."

Blackfire doesn't do anything, not at first. His tail is flat against his rump, and his ears are back. I can almost smell his fear. He waits until Hank is all the way out of the stall. Then he rushes outside at a gallop.

"He's so beautiful!" I exclaim.

"He is," Hank agrees. "I just hope I can get him calmed down so we can find a home for him."

"What if you don't?"

Hank stares out at the pasture, where Black prances, hooves bouncing as if the ground is made of sponge. "There's not much you can do when an abused horse won't come around. We couldn't sell him. And we couldn't keep him either. Gram would have to try to find somewhere that could take him and just leave him alone. Wouldn't be a good life, even if she did find somebody to take him on."

I'm afraid to keep asking the what-ifs, like what if nobody would take him on?

"Don't suppose you're up for mucking stalls?" Hank asks.

I'm pretty sure that means shoveling manure, and I'd much rather watch the horses. "Not today, if you don't mind. Maybe tomorrow?"

He laughs and goes back to Starlight's stall.

When he's out of sight, I sneak through Blackfire's stall and out to the pasture. Lancelot and Blackfire are grazing in one corner, keeping an eye on Starlight, who stands a few yards off.

Starlight trots toward the two horses. They stop eating and raise their heads to face the mare. When she's right up on them, they lower their heads and back away. Just a few steps, but they both do it. Then, as if she's satisfied, Starlight goes right back to where they were grazing just seconds ago.

It's hard not to think of the mare as a bully, but I try to remember what Winnie said in her e-mail. Horses need this structure. They need to know one horse is in charge. And I think I'm starting to see what she means. Lancelot and Blackfire go back to grazing. Gradually they move closer to Starlight and look more at ease. Instead of gawking around the pasture, they just eat.

I plop down in the grass and watch how the horses communicate with their bodies. Lance and Blackfire seem to know when it's okay to move past Starlight and when it's not. When Starlight faces them head-on, they stop or back off. If she turns and looks down, Blackfire strolls past her, unhurried.

I could watch them all day.

Hank finishes the stalls and comes to get me for breakfast. "What are you still doing out here?"

"Just watching," I answer.

"Funny." He shields his eyes in a salute as he gazes at the horses. "That's something Winnie would say."

When we walk into the kitchen, Kat's at the computer. She's back to her red, frizzy hair. This one is definitely a wig—can't believe I didn't see it before. Hair color is the only thing fake about this kid, and I'm betting she drops the whole thing before school starts. "Want to hear what Catman says about Kitten?"

"Sure." I pull up a chair. Popeye and Annie are eating breakfast together. Hank digs through cereal boxes. There's no sign of Wes, which is fine with me.

Kat reads Catman's e-mail out loud, and the guy sounds like a hippie in an old movie:

"Fight or flight, man! Those are Kitten's choices when she's spooked. So you got to read that cool cat of yours and know she's scared—before she scratches or runs. If her eyes get big, she's a scaredy-cat. If she narrows her eyes, she's trying to scare you back. Check out those groovy ears, man! Flat down, out to the side, scaredy-cat. Ears pinned back, she's trying to scare you. Read her whiskers. Pointed forward and up, she's scared. If she's nervous, she'll whip her tail low, back and forth. If she's really scared, she'll puff up her hair to look bigger."

Kat stops reading. "Isn't Catman the best? Hank says his cousin doesn't talk much in person, but he writes me long e-mails."

"So does he tell you what to do when Kitten gets scared?" I've read about horses' fight-or-flight reaction, and I'm wondering how much of this translates.

Kat turns back to the computer screen. "He says I should never stare at Kitten. And I can give her a 'cat kiss.'" Kat grins at me. "That's when you blink in slow motion at your cat, when she's looking at you."

Annie breaks us up because she has to leave for work. Kat follows her outside, which gives me a chance to check e-mail. I log in to my personal e-mail first. Neil has left me a message:

How are motor plans coming along?

Short and sweet. I dash off an answer, equally short and sweet:

Learning to drive a truck.

I log out of my own e-mail and go back to Annie's. Winnie left me another long e-mail.

It's even better than Catman's. It's as if Winnie has been watching the three horses with me. She describes the exact body language I observed. Then she tells me how to do the same thing, how to become Blackfire's leader. I try to memorize her instructions about using my own body language to communicate with the horse. She even gives me exercises I could do with Blackfire in Hank's round pen.

Popeye comes back in after seeing Annie off, and he looks like his mom just dropped him off for the first day of school.

Suddenly he straightens out of his slump and claps his hands. "As I recall, today is the beginning of Dakota Brown's career on wheels! Right this way!"

"Heads up!" Hank calls, tossing me a bagel. "Can't drive on an empty stomach."

I take a bite of the bagel and jog to catch up with Popeye, who's halfway to the truck already. "We'll just stay on the property for now," he explains. "After Saturday, when you pass the written driver's exam, we can venture out a bit."

"Driver's exam? Saturday?"

"You'll still have to take driver's ed in the fall."

109

I can't really tell him I don't need a permit since next week I'll be driving to Chicago without a license. I suppose it won't hurt to get the permit, though.

"You can study Hank's exam book," Popeye offers when we reach the truck. He opens the driver's door for me, and I slide in. By the time he gets in the other side, I have the key in the ignition.

"Not bad so far," he comments. "Except, aren't you forgetting something?"

I glance around the truck. "Where's the thingamadeal that moves the seat up?"

He shows me, and I adjust the seat. Then I fix the mirrors and get ready to turn the key.

Popeye stops me. "Ah-ah-ah. What are we forgetting?"

At this rate, our first driving lesson will take all day, and I won't even get to drive. "I give up."

"Rhymes with 'heat melt,'" he says, grinning.

I snap on my seat belt and wait for him to do the same.

For the next hour Popeye tells me—in excruciating detail—the nature of each of the truck's gears, the movements required for each gear, the road conditions that warrant shifting gears, and more hints than I could possibly use over the next 50 years.

By the time he actually lets me touch the accelerator, I'm seriously considering walking to Chicago.

Hank strolls up. "Safe to come out of the barn yet?"

"I think that's enough for lesson one," Popeye answers, cheerful as ever. "After lunch, we can pick up where we left off."

In the afternoon, Popeye gives me a driving demonstration, followed by pretend driving. We take a break, during which I watch Hank work with Lancelot. Then Popeye and I meet back in the truck, and I actually drive a few feet. Mastering the clutch and the gears is harder than I thought. The truck dies every few inches, but Popeye makes me hang in there. And by dusk, I'm able to make it out of first gear.

☆ ☆ ☆

On Friday, when Hank goes for a ride on his horse and Popeye takes off for a volunteer firefighters' meeting, I head straight for Blackfire's stall. He's not there, but I find him outside at the far end of the pasture, grazing with Lancelot.

I try calling Blackfire in from the pasture. He lifts his head but doesn't come. Snatching a handful of oats from the bin, I walk to the field, recalling Winnie's advice: Don't walk straight at him. Keep an eye on the other horses. Lower my eyes.

When I get close, I hold out the handful of oats, still not looking at him head-on. He stretches his neck like a giraffe to reach the oats. I could grab his halter and hope he'll let me lead him to the barn. But something inside tells me to try it the other way, to lead without a halter, as Winnie calls it.

Slowly, I square off in front of him and look directly at him as I raise my arms to my sides. He stops chewing and stares back at me. Then he lowers his head.

I turn, with my near shoulder moving forward. Then I look down, lower my arms, and walk toward the barn. *Please, make him follow me!* I'd say this is a wish, but I gave that up a long time ago. I think maybe it's a prayer, but I know I don't deserve to pray, because I only do it when I need something.

I'm afraid to look back. Then behind me comes the gentle *thud thump, thud thump* of hoofbeats. Blackfire is actually following me. He moves in so close I can feel his breath on my neck.

Only when we're in his stall do I turn around. "Good boy." I scratch his jaw where I know he likes it. "My good Blackfire."

I'd like to clean out his hooves, but I didn't think far enough ahead. Hank has hoof picks in the tack box, but I don't want to leave Blackfire and have him go back to the pasture. I could close him in the stall, but I don't want him thinking every time he follows me he'll end up trapped in a stall.

If I could get him to the round pen, I could close him in there and go get the pick. Then even if he chose "flight," he couldn't go far.

I repeat the same routine I did in the pasture. Again, Blackfire follows at my shoulder. He jumps a little when I unlatch the stall door leading into the barn, but he follows me out into the stallway, the aisle that runs in front of the stalls. He keeps trailing me all the way to the round pen area.

I can't even believe this is working so well.

We're about two feet from the pen's gate. Then we're home free.

"Hank?" Guinevere's shrill voice slices through the barn. Blackfire jerks to a dead stop.

"Come on, Blackfire," I coax, wishing I could tell Guinevere to shut up.

But it's too late. She walks into the barn, takes one look at me with Blackfire, and screams, "What are you doing with that horse? Get out of there!"

Blackfire rears, paws the air, then takes off at a dead gallop.

ELEVEN

BLACKFIRE KICKS UP his heels as he runs down one stallway, hits a dead end, and races back.

I'm so scared that it takes me a minute before I start after him.

"Don't get near that horse!" Guinevere shouts.

"Just shut up!" I holler back. I shouldn't shout either. It's probably the last thing Blackfire needs. But I'm so angry at Guinevere, I can't help it.

She's halfway up the ladder to the hayloft, staring down at me. "He could kill both of us!"

I try to block out her screeching voice and focus on calming Blackfire. He's trotting now, so I move to head him off. But he's so quick. He pivots left and canters by me.

Then I remember. *I'm* the leader. What would the lead horse do in a situation like this?

Calling up everything Winnie wrote about body language and everything I observed in the pasture, I make my move. This time as Blackfire races past me, I step in toward him. Shifting my shoulder forward, I walk with him a few steps. He speeds up, but this is what he should do. He runs in a rough circle around me.

When he comes around again, I move in and lift my arms slowly, as if blocking his way. I'm at least 12 feet from him, and he could still run wherever he pleases, but I can tell he's thinking it over. Does he want me to lead or not? I think he's going to bolt away again, so I stare into his eyes and lightly stamp my foot.

He freezes. We stand like that for what feels like hours, until he relaxes his neck and head. His shoulder muscles stop twitching.

Finally, I lower my arms and turn toward the round pen. Without looking back at him,

I start to walk, hoping—expecting—that he'll come with me.

He does. Blackfire follows me all the way into the pen. Once we're in, I latch the gate and take hold of his halter.

"It's okay, Guinevere," I call. "You can come down now."

Instead of Guinevere, Hank steps out of the shadows and moves toward us. Guinevere isn't far behind.

"Where did you learn to do that?" Hank asks.

My heart is pounding too loud for me to answer.

Hank walks up to the pen and stops on the other side of Blackfire and me. "You handled that just right, Dakota. Where did you learn how to advance and retreat like that?"

I shrug.

Hank shakes his head. "Let me get you a lead rope, and you can tie him in there. I'll get you a brush, too." He takes off toward the tack box.

"And a hoof pick?" I call after him.

"You're going to lift up his hooves?"

Guinevere says this as if I've announced my plan to perform brain surgery. On her.

"I guess."

"Fine." She starts to walk away. "But I'm bringing Lancelot in, so you better keep Black Devil away from him."

"His name is Blackfire!" I call after her.

She doesn't turn around. As she and Hank pass each other, though, she says something to him I can't hear.

"Brush," Hank says as he hands me one. "And hoof pick."

"Thanks."

He shows me where and how to tie the horse while I work on him. "Be good, Blackfire," he says before walking off.

Blackfire lets me brush him all over. When I get to his neck, he stretches, like I'm really scratching where it itches.

Hank helps Guinevere with Lancelot, then leaves us to groom our horses. We don't speak, so the only noise is *brush*, *swish*, *brush*. I move to Blackfire's left foreleg and trade in my brush for the hoof pick. As I bend down, I try to remember how Hank did it when he cleaned Starlight's hooves.

Blackfire's four hooves stay planted to the ground. I lift as hard as I can, but the hoof won't come up. I straighten and try to think like a leader. Force doesn't work. I need to ask. I take hold of the hoof again. "Could I please have your hoof now, Blackfire?" I ask politely.

When nothing happens, Guinevere sputters, apparently trying to hold in a laugh

I poke lightly just above Blackfire's hoof, while gently leaning against his shoulder. "Hoof, please?" When it doesn't come up, I press again, a little more firmly. And again. Then, miracle of miracles, Blackfire lifts his hoof.

"Thank you, boy," I say, trying to get a good hold on it. I scrape the pick around the hoof and in the V at the center. Then I move on. This time he gives me his hoof the first time I ask. Back hooves are tougher. I'm not sure how to hold them, but I give it a shot. When I set down the last hoof, I'm exhausted.

Guinevere makes a frustrated growl. "Get over, you big lug!"

I glance over and see her pushing on Lancelot's belly with both hands. She's wedged between the horse and the fence.

"You heard me!" she shouts, bracing her

back against the pen and leveraging her body to shove Lancelot sideways. "How do you expect me to brush this side if you won't . . . get . . . over?"

Lancelot seems to be ignoring her. His body sways slightly, then rebounds even closer to the fence than before she shoved him.

"Guinevere?" I pet Blackfire, then walk toward Lancelot.

"What?" She gives her horse another shove. He groans but refuses to budge. "This stupid horse. I'm telling Daddy I want that other horse he found for me. This one is too stubborn."

"You can't force him," I say, stroking the horse's neck.

"Fine. I just won't brush him then," Guinevere says. "But I still need to get him over so I can put on his saddle."

"Have you tried asking him? That touch-and-release thing really works."

"Wait a minute." She stops shoving Lancelot and pushes her hair out of her eyes. "Are you trying to tell me what to do with my own horse?"

"No. I just mean, if you didn't shove him—"

"Fine." She ducks under Lancelot's neck and comes around to my side. "You do it then."

"I don't know if I can do it or not," I admit.

"Really? I thought you said all I had to do was ask. Well, I'm asking you to ask."

Hank walks in with an English saddle and sets it over the pen rail. "What's up?"

"Dakota was about to show me how to make Lancelot move over for saddling."

I start to protest, but the truth is, I don't want her to shove the horse anymore. I slip to the other side, between fence and horse. "You're a good boy, Lance," I coo, scratching his withers. I hear Guinevere sigh, but I won't hurry.

I move my hand to his belly. "Okay, boy. Now I need you to move over."

He doesn't, and Guinevere laughs through her nose, a nose puff.

"Move, Lance," I say firmly. This time I barely poke his side. He sways but doesn't budge. "That's a boy. Move, please." I touch him again with my index finger. Then again. "There, now. Move." I keep steadily pressing, releasing, pressing.

And he steps aside.

"Good, Lancelot." I press again. But I don't

even need to this time. He moves all the way around.

Hank comes over and strokes Lance's head. "Good boy." He grins at me, and I grin back.

"Thanks," Guinevere says, taking her saddle off the fence. I'm not sure if she's thanking Hank for the saddle or me for the horse.

I go back to Blackfire while Guinevere saddles her horse. I don't think I'd like to ride with that puny saddle.

"Do you ride English?" Guinevere asks. She pulls the strap tighter and buckles it.

"No," I answer.

Hank hands her a bridle and holds Lance while she puts it on.

"That's too bad," Guinevere says, shoving the bit into Lance's mouth. Hank cringes. "Nearly all the good horse shows around here are English equitation."

"That's okay. I don't want to show." I can't imagine that being fun. And I'm sure *equitation* would make me want to hurl, even though I'm not exactly sure what it is.

"You do ride, though, don't you?" she asks.

"Yeah. Of course." Okay, so the truth is,

the only horse I ever rode was a plastic one in front of a grocery store. And nobody even put in the quarter to make it move.

"Why don't you saddle up?" Guinevere suggests. She turns to Hank. "Hank, can't you loan her a Western saddle?"

"No thanks," I say before Hank can answer. I have no more idea how to saddle a horse than I do how to cook one. "So not necessary."

"You ride bareback? Good for you!" she says with exaggerated sweetness. "Daddy won't let me." She gathers the reins in her left hand and stands beside the saddle until Hank cups his hands so she can use him as a stirrup. Once she's in the saddle, she says, "Hank, you have a bridle for Blackfire, don't you? Get it so Dakota and I can ride together."

Hank is way too used to taking orders from this girl. He smiles at me, then takes a bridle off the wall. My mind races, searching for another excuse for why I can't bridle this horse—an excuse that doesn't begin, "I'm so stupid, I don't know how to do this." But instead of bringing the bridle over, Hank disappears with it.

Thank you! Hank must have seen right through both of us females. Pretty hard to believe that Gwennie all of a sudden wants to be riding pals. Even harder to believe that Dakota Brown can ride a horse. My breathing slows to almost normal.

Hank reappears, leading Starlight by the bridle. "Sorry, I can't let you ride Blackfire," he says. "Not until I work him myself."

"Well, I guess I understand," I say, going for disappointed but brave.

"Are you sure you don't want a saddle, though?" he asks. He opens the gate and brings his horse into the pen.

"A saddle? No. That's okay." Maybe sometime I can practice saddling Blackfire, but I'll have to read up on it first. I back up to make room for Starlight. I'm pretty eager to get away from Guinevere, but I want to stick around and watch both of them ride first.

"Okay then." Hank leads Starlight over to me. "I still can't get over the fact that you ride. You'd think Ms. Bean would have been all over that. She acted like you'd never been around a farm or stable."

"Uh-huh." It's all I can say because my

mouth is as dry as Iraq. I'm getting the horrible feeling that Hank hasn't bridled Starlight for himself.

"Want a leg up?" He bends and cups his hands like he did for Guinevere. "Don't worry about her being blind. She's learned where the round pen is, even when she can't see it."

I can't just leave Hank with his stirrup hands, leaning over like that. I walk up and lift my right foot, until I figure out that would put me up backwards. Even I know I should face front. I shift, stick my left foot into Hank's hands-stirrup, and feel myself boosted up until I nearly flip over Starlight's back.

"Dakota, you okay?" he asks.

Before I can tell him, *No! I've never been less okay*, Guinevere rides past.

Starlight prances in place. Hank hands me the reins, but I'm not about to let go of the fat lock of mane I'm clutching in both hands. I couldn't unbend these fingers if my life depended on it. *Does my life depend on it?*

"Take the reins, Dakota," Hank urges.

I see the leather reins, knotted together and looped loosely around Starlight's neck. "No thanks," I say, squeezing my lock of mane.

I hear the clip-clop of Lancelot's hooves coming around again. Out of the corner of my eye, I see the rise and fall of Guinevere's black helmet. Why didn't I get a helmet? I'm the one who needs a helmet.

Lancelot swoops by us, and Starlight doesn't appreciate it one bit. She turns, ears back, and starts after the bay. Starlight the Dominant Mare does not like being behind.

"Whoa?" I cry, but my voice breaks and disintegrates in the sound of thudding hooves. Starlight wants the lead. She trots, only I don't post. I bounce. And bounce. My body jostles from side to side. The only steady contact I have with the horse is my fingers clutching her mane.

It's not enough. Up and down. The world is bouncing. Someone's shouting. My fingers are slipping.

And I'm sliding down,
                    down,
                         down. . . .

TWELVE

I HEAR MYSELF LAND with a thud a second before I feel the ground.

"Dakota!" Hank is running toward me.

Starlight stands over me, her head lowered, her muzzle inches from my nose.

Guinevere charges up on Lancelot, stops so short that dirt sprays, then jumps off. "Dakota? Tell me you're all right!"

"I'm all right," I repeat. I try to decide if I'm lying. But nothing hurts except my seat. I shake my arms, move my head. No problem.

"Hank," Guinevere says over my head, "I think something's wrong."

"Nothing's wrong." I let out the sound rising through my throat and discover it's a laugh. A giant, full-blown laugh that I can't control.

Hank and Guinevere stare at me as if I've lost my mind.

"That was so tight!" I exclaim. "I think that was the most fun I've ever had!" I burst into laughter again.

Hank has Blackfire tied just outside the pen, and I hear the horse sneeze. It sets me off all over again.

"Did she hit her head?" Guinevere sounds sincerely worried.

"I didn't hit anything," I say, my eyes watering from too much laughter. "Don't you get it? I just rode a horse. My first horseback ride. And my first fall. Yeah, they were only seconds apart, but–"

"You've never ridden before?" Guinevere demands.

"Have now," I answer.

"Dakota!" Hank locks his fingers behind his neck, and his face grows as red as Kat's wig. "Why did you say you've ridden before? I never would have put you on Starlight. And bareback?"

I reach up and stroke Starlight's soft muzzle. "She was wonderful! What a great horse for my first ride. Can we go again?"

"Not today," Hank says, sliding his hands under my arms and pulling me up. "Go inside and take care of that elbow."

My elbow looks dirty and bloody, but I'm still too high on horses to feel it.

I'm so caught up in the rush of my first horse ride, trying to relive the seconds I was actually on Starlight's back, that I don't see Wes as I come out of the barn. *Thunk!* We slam into each other, and I almost go down a second time. "Oops. Didn't see you there, Wes."

"Have you got it in for Taco, or what?" he demands. At Wes's heels, Rex starts barking.

Taco sticks his ratlike head out of Wes's denim jacket.

"Sorry. I didn't see the dog." But I can't afford to slip into defense with Wes. He's shaping up to be my opponent—his call, not mine. "*You* ran into *me*, by the way."

"What are you doing here, anyway?"

Rex barks louder, but not at me. He's barking at Wes. And the angrier Wes gets, the more Rex barks at him.

"Riding horses," I reply. It sounds so good that I have to fight off a grin.

"I don't mean *here*!" Wes shouts, pointing at the barn. "I mean *here*!" His arm sweeps the entire farm. "Why are you still here?"

I don't think there's any way he could have read my e-mails with Neil, so I act clueless. "I'm a foster, Wes, just like you."

"You're planning to bolt the minute you get the chance," Wes says. "I saw it in your eyes the day you got here."

I could deny it, but Wes knows. He knows, but he's not going to tell. Wes wants me out of here as much as I want out. "So why are *you* still here, Wes? Thought you said you were going back to live with your mother. Aren't *you* getting out of here?"

"Yeah. I was just hoping you'd be gone first." He brushes past me and into the barn, with Rex barking after him.

✳ ✳ ✳

"What did you do to your arm?" Kat rushes to me as if I've lost my arm instead of scraped my elbow.

130

"I'm fine, Kat. I rode a horse!"

Kat is less than impressed. She lifts my arm for a better look at the bleeding elbow. "We have to clean the wound."

It's hardly a wound. But I admit it's stinging now.

"Come on." Kat heads upstairs and I follow.

She leads me to our joint bathroom and makes me sit on the toilet lid while she digs through the medicine cabinet. She uses cotton balls to dab on rubbing alcohol, which stings like crazy. Then she puts on ointment and follows up with a bandage.

"Impressive, Kat," I say, meaning it. "Where did you learn all this?"

"Hospitals, mostly."

"So, are you going to be a doctor, like Annie?"

Kat shrugs. Then she coughs. She turns her head and keeps coughing for a solid minute.

"Kat? Want a glass of water or something?" I have no idea what to do.

Then, just like that, she stops. "Sorry about that. I'm fine. How's the elbow?"

I wave it like a chicken wing. "Good as new."

⋆ ⋆ ⋆

That night, my daring rise . . . and fall . . . on Starlight monopolizes dinner conversation. Wes stays out of it, but everybody else can't seem to let it go. I don't mind. I like reliving it. And Hank makes a big deal about how good I was with Blackfire, so it balances out.

Annie's quieter than usual. But when we get to dessert, she says, "So, Dakota, I hear you're taking your driver's exam tomorrow."

I'd almost forgotten about that. "Yeah."

"I was thinking," Annie says, "since I only work a half day on Saturdays, I could meet you after your exam. We could celebrate at the Made-Rite."

"Marvelous idea!" Popeye agrees.

"What if I flunk the test?" I ask.

"Then we'll have a pity party at the Made-Rite," Kat answers.

"Thanks for the vote of confidence, Kat." I elbow her. "Ouch." I connect right where I'm injured.

Wes is the first to leave the table. I'm next. I help clear, then head for the barn. When Hank comes in, I help him feed the horses and bed them for the night. The fresh hay smells like spring.

We walk back to the house together. The night is clear, and the sky is crowded with stars. I stop and stare up at them. "I've never seen stars like this." A curved path of stars crosses the sky. I point to it. "Hank, what's that?"

He squints at the sky. "Milky Way. And there's the Big Dipper." He points out a square of four stars, with a handle of stars. Then he shows me the Little Dipper and Orion, which is supposed to be some hunter guy with two dogs. It's hard to make it out, though. Hank knows a dozen constellations and tries to make me see them, but I can't quite put the pieces together.

"Don't worry about it," he says. "If you keep looking every night, it will start to make sense. Sometimes when I'm out here I think God put every star up there to remind me how big He is. Kind of cuts everything else down to size."

Hank hands over his driver's exam book, and I spend the rest of the night reading through it. There sure are a lot of rules to driving. Pretty soon I'm sick of reading about street signs and highways. I close my eyes, and my thoughts shift back to the barn. To horses and riding. I fall asleep dreaming about horses.

In the middle of the night, I wake up and can't fall back asleep. After fighting with the covers, I give up and turn on the lamp beside my bed, then grab my list-book and make a new list:

TOP 10 REASONS WHY HORSES ARE BETTER THAN CARS
1. Horses smell like heaven. Cars smell like oil and gas.
2. Horses feel softer.
3. Horses don't rust.
4. Hay is cheaper than gas.
5. Horses nicker softly. Cars honk loudly.
6. Horses will come when you call them.
7. Horses can follow you and let you be lead horse. (Who ever heard of a person leading a car?)
8. Horses interacting with horses are fascinating. Cars interacting with cars? That's a traffic accident.
9. Nobody has to take a driver's exam to ride a horse.
10. If you love a horse, I think the horse just might love you back.

Thirteen

Saturday morning I drag myself out of bed just as the sun is rising and get to the barn before Hank does. It's worth it when I see Hank's expression.

"Dakota Brown, you're full of surprises." He rips open a feed sack that smells like molasses and oats. "You feed Blackfire. I'll take Starlight and Lance. But no riding until we get you through your driver's exam."

I love watching Blackfire eat. He chews with his mouth closed, making every bite last.

I hang out with Blackfire until Popeye calls Hank and me back to the house.

Popeye is wearing slacks and a white shirt, and Kat has on nice jeans and a yellow top that matches her hair color of the day.

Popeye takes charge. "Kat, you get that driver's exam booklet. You can quiz Dakota on the drive up."

"Will we all fit in the truck?" I ask.

Popeye smiles. "Boys can ride in the back. Nice day like this."

Wes stands up from the computer chair. I hadn't even noticed him. "I don't want to go."

Popeye turns to him. "We're hitting the Made-Rite afterward."

"I need to make calls about Taco." He glares at me. "He still needs a good home."

"All right," Popeye says. "Just stay on the property. Don't watch television, of course. I'll leave my cell on in case you need us."

Wes nods, then bangs out the door with Rex at his heels.

Popeye stares after him. Then he wheels on me. "Dakota, get in gear! Let's see. Learner's permit. Can't remember how much that costs. You better bring 40 out of the pet bowl."

I have no idea what he's talking about. "Pet bowl? Forty what?"

"Dollars! We keep petty cash and money from pet adoptions in the pet bowl. Anytime we place a pet for a fee, the money goes for the good of all the animals. Below the sink. Blue bowl. Takeoff time in 10 minutes!"

I change into my nicest pair of jeans and a layered cami and tank. Then I race downstairs and find the pet bowl exactly where Popeye said it would be. There is nothing petty about the cash in this bowl. There must be a couple hundred dollars. I grab two 20s and run to the truck.

Hank climbs in the back, and I get into the cab with Popeye and Kat.

The trip to Nice flies by, with Kat quizzing me from the driver's booklet and Popeye tossing in random driving facts.

By the time we get to the DMV, I'm more nervous than ever about the test. Popeye parks, and we all walk in together. Hank's windblown hair would look better on a punk rocker.

Kat eases up beside me. "Don't worry. We'll pray for you while you're in there. Not that you'll magically get the answers right or anything."

"Awww," I say, acting disappointed.

"We'll just pray you remember the answers you do know," Kat adds.

They sit in the waiting room, taking up all but one of the remaining seats, while I go to the desk, pay the $20 fee, and fill out a form. When I'm done, I glance over at the waiting room. Hank, Popeye, and Kat each give me a thumbs-up.

Six computers line a back wall, where two other wannabe drivers are taking their exams. My hands shake as I slide onto the stool and try to listen to the examiner's instructions.

It doesn't take long to key in answers. I have to guess on a couple, but most of the questions are ones Kat asked me in the car. When I'm done, I wave at the examiner, then hold my breath while she grades my test.

Without a smile, she starts telling me about the state's driver's ed class, the number of driving hours required for a license, and other things that don't sink in.

"Did I pass?" I ask, interrupting her.

She grins and hands me a learner's permit. "Congratulations."

When I walk out to the waiting room, Popeye, Hank, and Kat stop talking.

I hang my head and shuffle over to them.

"Never you mind, Dakota," Popeye says.

"You can take the test as many times as you want," Hank adds.

Only Kat doesn't buy into this scene. "Dakota, did you pass?" she demands.

I sigh. Then I grin and wave the permit. "Yes!"

Before I know what's happening, the three of them are hugging me and dancing around like I've won the lottery. Even the two strangers in the waiting room clap for me.

As we walk back to the truck, Popeye bursts into a cheer: "Dakota, Dakota! She's smart like Quasimod-a!" He does a little tap dance and passes it to Kat.

Kat comes through with, "Dakota! Dakota! We'll celebrate with soda!" She does the same tap dance step Popeye did and passes it to Hank.

Hank's face reddens. He glances around the parking lot, then shakes his head.

"Come on, Hank!" Kat urges.

Hank rolls his eyes, then mutters, "Dakota, Dakota. Fight, fight, fight. Now let's go get some chow at the Made-Rite." Then he climbs into the back of the truck.

"Ouch," Popeye says, opening the cab door for us.

I slide in after Kat and try to remember if anybody has ever cheered for me before.

The Made-Rite restaurant isn't much bigger than a school classroom. Trailer-shaped, it has six stools at the counter, a big booth open on both sides in the back, another little booth in front, and three or four tables scattered in between. On the walls are framed ads from old magazines: the Campbell's soup kid, a Betty Crocker ad, and others I don't recognize. Country music blares from the kitchen.

"There she is!" Popeye says. He tucks in his shirt and runs his palm over his head.

We walk to the back booth, where a long-faced woman sits, her lips turned up slightly. She's wearing a light blue suit that matches her intense blue eyes—eyes that peer at me through wire-rimmed glasses. She's tall, at least sitting down, with short, curly blonde hair that I'm guessing should be gray.

"Mother!" Popeye scoots into the booth and kisses her on the cheek.

"Hi, Gram," Hank says, coming up beside me.

Kat scoots into the booth and kisses the woman's other cheek. "I've missed you, Gram."

"Gram" puts one arm around Kat, but she's still staring at me. "And you must be Dakota."

Hank and Popeye stumble all over themselves introducing me. "Dakota just passed her written driver's exam," Hank says, ushering me into the booth.

"Of course she did," Gram says, holding out her hand until I realize I'm supposed to shake it. "That is why we are here." She raises one finger and glances toward the counter.

"Coming, Mrs. Coolidge!" shouts the man behind the counter, a big man with a white apron and a three-cornered hat. He rushes four hot fudge sundaes to the table.

"Thank you, Marvin," Mrs. Coolidge says.

"Annie's not here yet?" Popeye glances around, looking dejected.

"She'll be here," his mother promises. Gram takes Kat's cheeks between her palms. "How are you feeling, my angel?"

"Good," Kat answers.

"When are you coming out to the Rescue?" Hank asks.

"She's way too busy for us," Popeye teases. "Unless she has a stray pet that needs a home."

"How can you say such a thing, Chester?" She sounds offended.

"I didn't mean it, Mother," Popeye says quickly. "I was just—"

She smiles at him, and I'm thinking she was teasing. But it's pretty hard to tell.

She stands, forcing Popeye to scoot out of the booth. "I do wish I could stay."

"You're leaving?" Popeye asks, standing back as she slides out of the booth.

"Duty calls," she replies. "Dakota, lovely to meet you. Hank, Katharine, a pleasure, as always." With that, she struts out, letting the screen door bounce behind her.

Popeye stares after her. "The woman is a force of nature," he observes proudly.

When we're halfway through our sundaes, Annie rushes in. She squints, finds us, then slides into the booth next to Popeye. "Well?" she asks, looking at me.

The others follow my lead and look sad.

"I never liked those driver's exams," Annie grumbles. "Well, we'll show 'em next time."

She looks so sad that I can't keep it up. "I passed."

She explodes with squeals that would get us kicked out of normal restaurants.

Popeye orders Made-Rites for all.

Annie glances around. "Where's Wes?"

"Didn't want to come," Popeye answers.

They exchange a look, then Annie changes the subject.

When my sandwich comes, they all watch until I take the first bite. My teeth sink into the softest bun, filled with meat like a hamburger that fell apart or a sloppy joe without the sauce. It comes with mustard on the bottom and ketchup on the top, and it just might be the best sandwich in the entire world.

Marvin, the owner, gives us a lot of special attention, including extra pickles and fries. When he brings me another Made-Rite, on the house, Popeye asks him to sit down with us.

"Fourth of July's fast approaching," Popeye says.

"A week from today," Marvin adds. "You coming in for the fireworks?"

"Wouldn't miss it," Hank says, taking a bite of his own Made-Rite.

"We'll be celebrating a triple birthday!" Popeye exclaims.

"Hank, Dakota, and America," Kat explains.

Suddenly, I can't eat. I have no business being here with this family. I won't be here for the triple birthday. I don't want to imagine what they'll think when they find out I've run off to LA.

I listen quietly as they make their big plans.

"Don't forget Ms. Bean and her young man will be here," Annie says.

Marvin promises a giant cake and plenty of Made-Rites.

When we leave and walk outside, Hank looks around. "Mom, where did you park your car?"

Annie points to a gold Plymouth minivan.

"You got it!" Popeye hugs her. "Any problems?"

Annie shakes her head.

"But where's *your* car?" Kat asks.

"Our family is getting too big for a sports

car," Annie says. She dangles her keys. "So, who's riding with me?"

We divide up, girls in the van, guys in the truck.

⭐ ⭐ ⭐

When we're back at the farm, I check e-mail and find a long message from Winnie. She gives me advice on riding and staying on. At the very end, she closes with this:

Take your time with Blackfire.

But what she doesn't know is that I don't have time to take.

FOURTEEN

SUNDAY MORNING Kat wakes me up way too early, and we all go to church in the new van. Their church could be a Christmas card. Small and white, old-fashioned steeple, evergreens everywhere. Only thing missing is the snow.

When I step out of the van, I expect to hear organ music. Instead, I hear drums and horns and a tambourine. I can't believe these sounds are coming from a church.

"Nice, huh?" Hank says, weaving to the beat.

We sit in a long pew, with Wes taking one end and me the other. Kat sits next to me.

She looks up every Bible verse and holds her Bible between us like we're sharing. A lot of the talk—or the sermon, I guess—goes over my head. But the music rocks. I had no idea Jesus songs could sound like that.

✱ ✱ ✱

When we get back to the farm, Popeye fixes grilled cheese sandwiches. Then he gives me a driving lesson in the truck.

"Clutch!" Popeye cries, as we inch along the pasture trail.

But it's too late. I stall out the truck for the 13th time. "I'm never going to get it," I complain.

"*Never* is never a word to use under these circumstances," he says. "Let's go again."

We do. I stall the truck four more times. But I'm starting to get the hang of steering. I have a long way to go before I can take this thing to Chicago.

When we're done, Popeye rushes inside to help Annie bake cookies. I head for the barn and Blackfire. Hank's working with Lancelot in the round pen. I watch them as I groom Blackfire.

"Lancelot's looking good," I tell Hank when he comes by again. "He seems more relaxed." I'm pretty sure Hank's working him with a different bit.

"He's coming along," Hank says. He stops beside Blackfire and me.

I run the brush all the way to Blackfire's hooves. "Of course, Lance might do better if he had another horse riding with him."

Hank laughs. "If you think I'm putting you back up on Starlight, you're crazy."

"Actually, I was thinking of Blackfire." I expect Hank to laugh even harder, but he doesn't.

I figure he's rejected my idea, though, since he dismounts and unsaddles Lancelot. He flings the saddle over his shoulder and heads for the tack room.

I move over to Lance and start brushing him. His back is damp from the saddle, so I brush it the wrong way, then back again.

Finally Hank returns. He watches me with Lance for a few minutes. Then he sighs. "Okay. Only not by yourself. I lead him."

"Yeah? Seriously?" I can't believe Hank's going to let me ride Blackfire.

149

"You just sit there. I'll do everything else. I mean it, Dakota. I don't want you falling off again."

"Me either," I agree. I walk over to Blackfire and put my arms around his neck. "Ready, handsome?" I whisper. "We're going on a ride."

Hank takes Lance to his stall and comes back with a Western saddle, the kind cowboys use in movies. He shows me how to place the saddle blanket and where to cinch the saddle.

Blackfire's back twitches when we tighten the girth, but he doesn't try to get away.

"Are you sure this saddle's comfortable for him?" I don't like the way the horse keeps turning his head to look at it.

"As comfortable as a 25-pound chunk of leather can be on your back, I guess," Hank says, pulling the cinch two notches tighter than I had it.

Hank teaches me how to mount, and it's much easier with a real stirrup and a horn to grab on to. "Ready?" he asks, as I settle into the saddle.

I nod. My heart is racing. At first, I hang on to the horn while Hank leads me around the pen. Then I let go and feel my body move with Blackfire's stride.

Still, I can't feel the horse like I could when I rode Starlight bareback. "Hank?"

"What?"

"Do you think I could ride bareback?" I ask.

"You're kidding. Remember what happened last time?"

"But I want to feel Blackfire. I think I need to feel him. Please?"

Hank stops, and so does Blackfire. When Hank stares at me, I think this could go either way. "You sound just like Winnie. You know that?"

"I do?" Right now, on horseback, there's nobody else I'd rather sound like.

"Winnie loves to ride bareback." Hank scratches his head, then sighs. "Okay."

Blackfire seems more relaxed the second the saddle comes off. Hank boosts me up, and I settle onto the horse, feeling more a part of him this way. I know it will be harder to stay on without a horn and stirrups. But Blackfire's not as broad-backed as Starlight, so it's easier to grip with my thighs.

Hank leads me, and I cling to a fistful of mane. But after once around, I loosen my grip and rely on my legs to keep me on. I lose track of how many trips we take in the round pen. When we quit, I slide off and hug Blackfire.

"There's hope for you yet," Hank mutters.

I don't know if he's talking about Blackfire or me.

I run inside and tell Kat about riding Blackfire. Then I log on to Annie's e-mail and get ready to write Winnie. But Winnie has beat me to it. There's a message waiting with the subject line: *Fight or Flight*.

I read through it. It's the same kind of thing Catman told Kat about cats. Horses are "prey" instead of predators. So when they get frightened, their instinct is to fight or run away, and almost always, they'll choose to run away.

If you can just remember that a horse's first reaction to anything new is to run away, you'll go a long way toward understanding Blackfire.

I can't help smiling to myself. Maybe that's why Blackfire and I have understood each other from the beginning. Running away is something I've always understood.

I start upstairs, but Kat meets me on her way down. "Come on!"

"Come on where?"

"Sunday night stargazing," Kat answers. "Didn't anybody tell you?"

I shake my head.

Hank comes thundering down the stairs, and even Wes heads for the lawn, where Annie and Popeye are spreading out blankets.

I follow along and take a spot next to Kat. For the rest of the night, under bright starlight, we watch the sky and eat popcorn to the tune of crickets, hoot owls, and an occasional woodpecker.

☆ ☆ ☆

The next morning, I'm ready for another driving lesson. But when I come downstairs, Popeye's chugging a glass of milk as he stands over the sink. He's wearing brown pants and a matching jacket that says "Nice Fire Dept."

When he sees me, he says, "Good, you're

up, Dakota. I'm due at the fire station. One of the boys called in sick."

Annie's stuffing papers into her briefcase. "Morning, Dakota. Sorry we have to rush off like this."

"When are you coming back?" I ask, hoping it will be in time to give me another driving lesson.

"Up to my chauffeur," Popeye answers, switching his lunch bag to his teeth so he can open the door for his wife.

"Great," I mutter when they're gone. "Now what am I supposed to do?"

Hank gets up from the table and sets his dishes in the sink. "How about riding Blackfire?"

Suddenly I'm not so disappointed. "Seriously? Yeah!"

I ride bareback, and again Hank leads me around the pen. After the fourth round, I'm ready to move on. "Hank, you can let go now. We'll be fine."

He steps back and holds up both hands. "I haven't led you for the last two laps."

"Then scram. Blackfire and I want to be alone."

"Guess I can take a hint." Hank leaves the

ring but watches from the side as Blackfire and I continue to walk around and around. Finally, even Hank seems to get bored. "I'm going to muck stalls," he says. "Call me if you need me."

After a couple more laps, I'm getting dizzy, and I think Blackfire must feel the same. He edges closer to the pen. This time, when we pass the open gate, it's like Blackfire's reading my mind. He tucks, turns, and walks out of the pen.

I don't try to rein him back. I want to see where he'll go. Unhurried, he crosses the barn to the barn door, then out into the beautiful sunshine.

This is riding. I breathe deeply, and the air smells clean. I glance around and see Kat waving at me from the front window.

Blackfire stops, and I wave back at Kat.

Out of nowhere comes a growl. Then a *yap, yap, yap!*

"Taco!" Wes comes running from the house. "Get back here!"

But the little dog keeps running, making a beeline for Blackfire's hind legs.

Suddenly, Blackfire lets out a whinny. The dog yaps at his heels. I feel the horse gather himself under me. Then he lunges.

I grasp at his mane to keep from falling off. Blackfire takes off, and I'm thrown forward so that I'm hanging on to his neck. He takes this as a sign to speed up.

We thunder up the hill. We're halfway through the next field before I remember to breathe.

I'm surprised to feel the reins still in my hand. Somebody's yelling behind me, but I can't make out the words. I scoot back into riding position and remember to grip with my thighs.

The rhythm of the gallop begins to take me with it, regular and steady. Up and back. I loosen my grip on his mane, feel the wind on my face, and move with Blackfire. He runs across the road, and I'm with him, beat for beat. I'm not afraid. I want us to keep running together. Forever. Just like this. No wonder we're riding as if we're one. He's running away, and that's what I do best.

Ahead of us, I see rocks piled high.

We close in on the mound. But the closer we get, I see more rocks. And something else. It's a quarry—a deep, cavernous quarry.

And we're headed straight for it.

FIFTEEN

I SIT UP AS STRAIGHT as I can on Blackfire's back until I can see the giant hole in the ground, the quarry that's getting closer with every hoof-beat. I picture us galloping over the side, flying, then crashing down . . .

"Whoa!" I shout, pulling back on the reins. I remember what Winnie said about ask and release. So I pull, let up, then pull.

Blackfire puts on the brakes so fast I almost sail over his head. But I catch myself. "Good boy!" I stroke his sweaty neck and ease my seat behind the withers. We're both panting. I don't think I've ever felt this alive. Even as I think this, I know it sounds like a soap opera, but there it is—that feeling. In my soul, like Popeye and his woodpeckers.

I lay the reins on Blackfire's neck, and he turns around and starts walking back to the barn as if our ride were nothing more than a little exercise. Halfway there, I hear shouts. Hank's running toward us, waving his arms. He stops when he sees us walking toward him. He leans over, hands on knees, like he's trying to get his breath.

Wes catches up to Hank the same time I get there and frowns up at me. Then he turns around and heads back to the barn.

Hank inspects Blackfire and me. "You sure you're okay, Dakota?"

I lean forward and hug Blackfire around the neck. "Hank, I've got to tell you. That was more fun than falling off Starlight."

✳ ✳ ✳

Next morning there's an e-mail waiting for me:

Can you drive yet?

Neil always was a man of few words.

But the message hits hard. Right now there's no way I could drive that truck to Chicago. I can't even make it across the pasture without stalling out. I need more practice.

I don't answer Neil's e-mail.

I look around for Popeye, who never sleeps in—and "sleeping in" means anything after seven. There's a note on the table, anchored under the sugar bowl. I move to the table to read it:

Fire duties. Gone with Mac. Digging trenches near Marengo. Back later.
Love,
Popeye/Chester/Dad

Great. There goes my driving lesson. In four days I'll be on the road to Chicago. I'm running out of time. And patience.

By four o'clock, Popeye still isn't back. I've ridden Blackfire, checked e-mail, and scouted the driveway for any sign of Popeye. With nothing else to do, I stroll around the barn and see the truck's still parked where I left it. Mac, a neighbor and fellow firefighter, must have given Popeye a lift.

I think about asking Hank if he'll give me a driving lesson, but he's out riding Starlight. I stare at the old truck, knowing that in a few days I'll be driving it by myself.

So why not now?

The key's right where it always is. I snap on my seat belt, and the truck starts with the first try. Gears grind as I wiggle the stick to first. The truck jerks, but it doesn't die. I head for the path along the back field and bounce through the pasture with no problem. This is by far the best I've driven. At the end of the field, the gate's missing. So I keep going down a little incline and onto the road.

It's easier than I thought, driving on a gravel road. Pressing the accelerator and picking up speed, I try to imagine myself on the expressway. Actually, it's easier to stay straight at this speed than when Popeye makes me dog it. I pass the Coolidges' driveway and keep going until I come to a crossroad. Dust clouds rise from both sides as I turn left and regain speed. I'm guessing it's a country mile to the next intersection when I turn left again. The corner comes a little fast, and I turn too sharply, but nobody's coming.

I settle into the seat again and relax my hands on the wheel. I can do this. I really can. As soon as I get back, I'll e-mail Neil and tell him. I take another left at the intersection, then another, and I'm pretty sure I'm back on the road I started on. Nobody else is out here. I own the road.

I whiz past the horse pasture. Then, out of the corner of my eye, I see the Coolidges' driveway. It's up on me sooner than I thought, so I have to wheel right to make the turn.

In front of me, tiny eyes shine up from the road—a raccoon or a rabbit. I swerve to miss it. But the truck goes too far too fast.

My front tire bumps off the drive, and I can't get it back. I'm going too fast. I yank the wheel the other way. Back tires spin. I jerk the steering wheel, but nothing happens.

I hear a scream. It's me. I'm the one screaming. The truck's heading straight for a tree. I close my eyes. Then I hear the crash.

My body lunges forward, then jerks back from the seat belt.

When I open my eyes, I'm looking at a tree. Branches are pressed against the cracked windshield, like an old man's fingers trying to get in. I'm still squeezing the steering wheel. I've gripped it so hard, my fingernails are broken. I wiggle my fingers, move my arms. Nothing else seems to be broken.

Except the truck.

The giant trunk of the tree is so close I could reach out and touch it, which means the whole front part of the truck has been squished like an accordion.

The Coolidges are going to kill me.

I lean back in the seat, amazed that I don't hurt. My heart sounds like galloping horses' hooves, but I'm okay. I don't see blood anywhere.

That's when I realize somebody's honking. The steady cry of the horn blares through the dusk. I look around for another car, then figure out that it's the truck's horn. It's stuck. I pound on it until it cuts off, leaving an eerie silence.

The driver's door swings open, and Hank's there. "She's okay!" he shouts. He reaches in and tries to pull me out, but the seat belt's still fastened. He undoes the belt, then slides one arm under me and lifts me out of the truck.

Kat rushes up and grabs my arm. She's sobbing. "Dakota! Are you hurt?"

"I'm okay, Kat." I see Wes behind her, and he looks scared. Then I look at Hank, who's still holding me like I'm a baby. "You can put me down, Hank."

"Sure?" Hank holds me a few seconds longer, then sets me down.

My left knee hurts when I try to stand. It buckles, and Hank reaches for my arm to steady me.

A van pulls up behind us, and both doors spring open. Annie and Popeye come running for me. "Dakota!" Popeye shouts. The headlights point bright fingers at me through the settling dusk.

Annie says something I can't make out.

I brace myself. I don't think they'll hit me. But they'll go ballistic as soon as they see their truck. I try to stand up straight and get ready.

Annie reaches me first. "Dakota! What did you do? Are you okay?"

Then Popeye's there. He puts his hand on my head. His mouth opens, but nothing comes out.

Annie kneels down, even though she's wearing a white skirt. "What did you do to your knee? Let me see." Gently, Annie squeezes my kneecap and pokes and prods. When she stands, she lets out a sigh. "Well, nothing's broken that I can see. You'll have a nasty bruise though." She peers into my face. Then she feels my arms.

Popeye looks up at the sky. "Thank You, Lord!"

"Man," Hank says, more to them than to me. "I heard this bang, then a crunch. Then Kat came running into the barn to get me."

"It was so scary," Kat says, still looking stunned.

Wes hasn't left, but he stands to one side.

Popeye throws his arm around Kat. "It's over now. Everything's just fine."

This is *so* not the reaction I expected. "Your truck," I say. "It's wrecked."

"What about her knee?" Popeye asks, peering down as if he hasn't heard me. "Sure it's not broken?"

"Am I sure it's not broken?" Annie repeats. "Have you seen my medical degrees, Mr. Coolidge?"

They both laugh.

None of this makes sense. I feel like I'm watching these people from another dimension. "Hey! I wrecked your truck!" I shout. "*I did it. I drove by myself, and I smashed your truck into a tree.*"

The smiles don't disappear from their faces. "We love *you*, not that truck," Popeye says.

"What?" I don't believe he just said what he did.

"We're just grateful you're okay," Annie begins. "Of course, you shouldn't have been driving on your own."

Here it comes, I think. Now I'm going to get their *real* reaction.

"True," Popeye agrees. "We have time to come up with something."

Annie smiles at me, then squints like she's concentrating. "Dakota doesn't watch TV like Wes does, so that won't work. Extra chores maybe?"

That's it? Extra chores? "Don't you get it?" I shout. Only now do I feel tears pushing to get out. "I wrecked your truck! I'm sorry. I'm really sorry! But I can do extra chores until I'm a hundred, and I still won't have the money to pay you back!" Tears stop up my throat, and I cough.

"It will all work out," Popeye says.

"No, it won't!" I want them to be angry, to yell at me, to hate me for this. "I'll never be able to pay you back."

"We know," Annie says.

"Dakota," Popeye says, "most of what we do, we can't pay back."

"That's why we need Jesus," Kat whispers.

I'm out of words. Out of breath. Out of everything.

"I could sure use some hot chocolate," Hank says, sticking out an elbow for me to lean on.

I do lean on him and hobble to the house, but I skip the hot chocolate.

From my hot, bubbly bath, I listen to the laughter rise from downstairs, the voices seeping up through the radiator vents.

Sleep comes easily. But in the middle of the night I bolt upright in bed. *There's no truck!*

No truck means nothing to drive. Nothing to drive means no Chicago. No Chicago means no California.

I throw off my covers and hobble barefoot

down the stairs. My knee hurts, but I ignore it. The computer's turned off, and it takes forever to warm up. I log on to my e-mail and dash off a message in all caps, slapping *READ THIS NOW!!!!* in the subject line.

NEIL, HELP! I WRECKED THE TRUCK!

I CAN'T DRIVE TO CHICAGO.

YOU HAVE TO COME HERE AND GET ME!

★ ★ ★

I try to go back to sleep, but I can't. Pieces of the last two days fly through my head like runaways: my wild ride on Blackfire, the truck slamming into the tree, Popeye placing his hand on my head.

Why don't they hate me for wrecking their truck? I don't understand. And I don't belong. Not with these people. Not with this "Nice" family.

I belong with Neil. And DJ. And whoever and whatever's waiting in California. Not here, where people don't get mad at you for wrecking their truck, where they say they love you when they should hate you.

When it starts getting light outside, I give up trying to sleep and go back down to the computer. Maybe Winnie sent me more horse e-mails. I log in to Annie's e-mail account and scroll down, looking for something from Winnie.

An e-mail catches my eye. But it's not from Winnie. It's from someone named George. Addressed to Annie. The header reads: *We need to meet!*

I know I shouldn't, but I click on the e-mail and read:

My dearest Annie,

We cannot go on like this. It's been days since our last encounter. We must meet. You must tell your husband. I need you more than that husband of yours needs you. I miss you madly.

All my love,

George

SIXTEEN

THE SCREEN DOOR SLAMS, and I jump up from the computer as if I've been shot.

It's Wes and Rex. Rex trots over to me and wags his tail until I pet him.

Wes, still in pajamas, eyes me suspiciously. "Great job on the truck," he says. "Guess that makes it a little harder to run away."

I don't answer him. I couldn't speak if I wanted to.

He walks past me and goes back to bed.

I feel sick inside. The words in George's e-mail race through my brain, electrically charged. How could Annie do this to Popeye?

He loves her so much. *His* Annie. Right. What a lie.

Love? If that's where love gets you, then I want out more than ever.

I can't wait for Neil to write. I know it's too early to call him, but that's just too bad. And I know I'm not supposed to make long-distance calls without asking. But it seems to me there are a lot of things being done around here that are not supposed to be done.

I pick up the phone and dial Neil's number.

The phone rings six times, and I'm afraid nobody's going to answer when somebody finally does. "Who is this?"

I'm pretty sure it's not Neil's voice. "Uh . . . is Neil there?"

The guy swears under his breath. Neil lives with two other guys, but this doesn't sound like either of them. Then I wonder if it's DJ.

I wait so long I think about hanging up. Then Neil answers. "Who is this?"

"Neil, it's me. Dakota."

"What's the matter?"

"I wrecked the truck I was going to drive to Chicago."

"You're kidding. You better have a backup plan. Are they ready to kill you, or what?"

"Not exactly." I picture Annie running up to me to see if I was okay. But I shove the image from my head and instead try to imagine her with George.

"Dakota?" Neil says. "You still there?"

"Neil, you have to come get me."

In the background, I hear somebody yell.

"Was that DJ?" I ask.

"Yeah. And he's not going to want to drive all the way out to get you. That costs money, Dakota. Gas prices are killing us already."

"Well, what am I supposed to do?" I can't stop my voice from cracking. I'm on the verge of an all-out cry.

"Let me think," Neil says. His sigh travels through the phone.

I wait. "Please, Neil."

"Do you have any money? Maybe if I told DJ you could pay your own way . . ."

"I only have $10," I admit.

"There's got to be money around there somewhere, Dakota."

"You want me to steal?" I've never stolen

171

anything, not even when kids copped gum from the supermarket.

"Borrow, then," Neil says. "Anyway, they owe us. Fosters, I mean. They're getting money for you. From the state. And they've probably got you doing farmwork without pay too, right?"

"I don't know, Neil." And I don't. I don't know what to think or believe or do.

"Get the money, kid," Neil says. "I'll talk to DJ. You better overnight the cash, though. I think if he sees a hundred bucks, he'll do it."

"But I haven't said I'd–"

"Mail it to me here. Fast. We need to get it by Friday."

My head hurts. I just want to go to sleep and not wake up. I can't handle any of this.

"Dakota?" Neil's voice is wide awake now. He sounds as sure and confident as I am unsure and confused. "Listen to me. You don't belong there. We'll get jobs in LA. DJ's got us covered. Just get the money and send it to me. You hear me, Dakota?"

"Yes."

"Good. I'll see you on the Fourth. Everything will be all right." Neil hangs up.

I'm shaking when I hang up the phone. My breathing is jagged, like a bunch of spikes are cutting up my insides with every breath. I stand and walk to the kitchen. I open the cupboard under the sink. The pet bowl's there, loaded with cash.

But I can't do it. I can't take that money.

I slam the cupboard and race back upstairs. I have to get out of here. But there has got to be another way. I storm into the bathroom before I realize someone's already there.

"Oops. Sorry, Kat. I didn't—"

Kat is standing over the sink, staring at herself in the mirror. Or rather, staring at me staring at her. Kat is bald. There's not a hair—not a red, black, or blonde hair—on that pale, shiny head.

"One day," Kat begins, as if she's starting a fairy tale, "I looked in this mirror, and I only had three hairs. So I said, 'Hmm. I think I'll braid my hair today.' And I did. The next day I looked in this mirror, and I only had two hairs. So I said, 'Hmm, I think I'll part my hair down the middle today.' The next day I looked in the mirror, and there was only one hair on my head. So I decided on a ponytail. The next day I looked in this mirror, and there wasn't a single hair on my head." She turns to me and smiles. "Know what I said?"

I shake my head.

"'Finally! No more bad hair days.'"

I don't laugh. I can't. No more than I can stop staring at her head, the way the veins curl close to the skin.

"It's okay, Dakota. It really is."

"It's not okay." Tears are flooding my eyes and overflowing onto my cheeks. "Why? What happened to you? What's . . . ?" I don't even know what to ask her.

"I have cancer. If I didn't, I never would have met Mom. My biological mother couldn't handle it when I got sick."

"You can't have cancer, Kat."

"Don't look so scared, Dakota. Everything will be all right."

I back away from her. How can she say everything will be all right? That's what Neil said on the phone. I replay Neil's voice in my head and hear his words: *Everything will be all right.*

Then, before the sound of his voice can fade back into Kat's, I run downstairs, go to the pet bowl, and take out all the 20s, seven of them: $140.

The money feels warm in my fingers. I'll pay them back. I'm borrowing, not stealing. Dakota Brown is not a thief. *"Everything will be all right."*

Frantically, I search through the computer desk until I find a drawer full of envelopes and stamps. There's an overnight express mailer, but I have no idea how much it costs to send it. So I stick stamps all across the top, making a mental note to pay Popeye back for this, too. I scribble the return address on the envelope. Neil can find me from that.

Then, before I change my mind, I run outside, barefoot, all the way to the mailbox, stick in my package, and put up the red flag.

I run back to my room and stay upstairs until I'm sure Annie's gone. When I come down, Popeye's whistling one of the songs they sang in church.

If he only knew.

Knowing about Kat somehow makes me angrier at Annie. The famous Dr. Annie Coolidge should have cured her. They should have told me about Kat.

Popeye turns as if he's just noticed me. "You just missed Miami! How's the knee?"

I've been so upset that I've forgotten about my bruised knee. It hurts, but it's nothing compared to what I feel inside. "Fine."

"I knew it," Popeye says, pouring me a glass of juice when I sit at the table. "Miami is the best doctor in the world. She is never wrong."

"She's not perfect, Popeye." It comes out louder than I meant it to.

Kat's coming down the stairs, holding on to her kitten. She's wearing the red hair she wore the first day I got here.

"No," Popeye admits, "I suppose she's not perfect."

He and Kat exchange good-morning hugs, and then Kat moves to the TV and turns on some stupid cartoon show.

Popeye goes back to whistling as he mixes dough in a bread machine. He is so out of touch. His own wife is making a fool of him, and he's baking her fresh bread.

"Annie can't even cook, can she?" I point out.

He shakes his head and grins at Kat.

"Now, that's a fact. And you're very lucky she quit trying."

"She's always gone too," I add. "You do everything around here. She leaves her stuff all over the house, and you clean up after her."

With each fault I bring up, Popeye's grin becomes bigger, deeper. He gets this dreamy look in his eyes. "I do love that woman's faults. Maybe most of all."

He is so clueless. "Popeye! How can you?"

"It's those faults that got me Miami. Without them, she'd have gotten a much better husband than me. I'm a one-woman man, Dakota."

It's no use. I can't even imagine what it will do to him when he finds out about George. But it's not my problem.

Kat comes over and sits in the computer chair. "Dad, tell Dakota how you're a gecko."

"A gecko?" I repeat.

"But not just any gecko," Popeye says. "Most geckos have harems. But I'm like the Madagascar day gecko. He mates for life. If his wife dies, the poor fellow wanders around for the rest of his life, a dejected widower."

None of this is my problem. None of it.

I get up and go outside without a word, and I don't come in until it's time for supper.

Annie arrives home late, and Popeye keeps dinner waiting for her. She monopolizes the dinner conversation, talking about how great she is with her patients.

After dinner, she smiles at me before I can get away. "How's the knee?"

I turn away without answering her.

"Something wrong, Dakota?" Annie asks. "You were awfully quiet at dinner."

"Well, *by george*, what could possibly be wrong in this *loving* household?" I ask sarcastically. I leave before I say anything else.

SEVENTEEN

POPEYE SUGGESTS A TRIP into town for ice cream, and everybody but me races for the new van. I pull out my headache excuse, then have to convince Kat to go without me.

They've been gone about a half hour when the phone rings. It rings and rings since they don't have voice mail or an answering machine like normal people. There's a chance it could be Neil.

I dash out of my room and grab the upstairs phone. "Hello?"

"H-hello?" It's a man, but it's not Neil. "Uh . . . is Annie around? I need to talk to her about a meeting."

Right. Just like in the e-mail. This has got to be George. I picture him—tall, handsome, not bald.

"Excuse me? Would you please get Annie Coolidge for me," he says, as if he has a right to talk to her, to do whatever he wants, no matter who gets hurt.

"Annie doesn't live here anymore." And with that, I hang up on him. Hard.

☆ ☆ ☆

I have to wait until Friday before I hear from Neil. He got the money. He and DJ will be at the farm at five o'clock the next day. The rest is up to me.

I spend the whole day with Blackfire, grooming and riding, saying secret good-byes in my heart. Hank tries to talk to me a couple of times, but he gets the hint and keeps his distance.

At dusk I'm walking back to the house when Annie drives up. She honks, but I ignore it.

As soon as we're all sitting down for dinner, Annie asks, "Did anyone take a phone call for me Wednesday night?"

I stare at my plate.

"What do you mean?" Kat asks.

"My boss, Dr. Ramsey, said he called the house and somebody told him I don't live here any longer."

I knew George was a doctor.

"Maybe he got a wrong number," Hank suggests.

Nobody talks much the rest of the meal.

I've worked out every detail of my escape except for one, and I keep turning over this last problem in my head. Neil and DJ are coming straight to the farm. That's good because all the Coolidges will be in Nice. The problem is, how am I going to get them to leave *me* on the farm alone? I could fake a headache, but somebody might insist on staying with me. Or they might cancel the celebration altogether.

"What time's the parade tomorrow?" Kat asks.

"Not until four," Popeye answers. "I need to go into town early, though. Promised to drop off some equipment at the firehouse."

"We'll have to go in two cars, then," Annie says. "I need to see old Mrs. Elmer in the morning." Then, as if she just remembered they no longer have two cars, she adds, "Maybe your mother could come by and pick you up."

I've been tuning Annie out all night, but now I'm all ears.

"We could meet at the parade," Popeye suggests. "Or the Made-Rite afterward, if we miss each other. We want to get to the park in time to get good seats for the fireworks."

"Can I go with you to the station, Dad?" Hank asks.

"Sure," he answers.

"Me too?" Wes asks.

"Works for me. I'll call Mother and make sure she can swing by and get us."

"I'll go with you, Mom," Kat volunteers. "It'll be a pretty long day if I go with Dad." She turns to me. "Will you come with us? Just us girls?"

I start to say, "No way!" but then it hits me. This is my way out. "Okay."

And the last detail of the plan has just slipped into place.

✷ ✷ ✷

I spend the rest of the night packing. It seems like a year since I unpacked these same bags.

182

Outside, there's a loud *Pop! Pop! Pop!* I've never understood the fuss about fireworks. I used to hear the same sound some nights when I lived behind the Yards in the south side of Chicago.

With nearly everything packed, I sit on my bed and pull out my list-book. Then I start a new list:

TOP 10 THINGS I WON'T MISS ABOUT STARLIGHT ANIMAL RESCUE
  1. Annie's lies
  2.

Ten minutes later, that's all I have.

There's a knock at my door. I shove my suitcases into the closet and go see who it is.

Kat's standing there, her face pale and her mouth a straight line of worry. "Did Kitten come up here?"

I shake my head. "Why?"

"She got scared. Wes set off a firecracker, and Kitten took off running."

"She'll turn up, Kat."

Kat nods. "Yeah. I guess." But her forehead is as wrinkled as an old woman's. She walks down the hall, calling, "Here, Kitten, Kitten."

In the morning, July 4, I wake up with a sick feeling in my stomach. I try to convince myself I'm just excited about leaving, excited about seeing Neil and starting a new life in California.

Everybody except Kat is eating breakfast when I come downstairs. They shout, "Happy birthday!" to me and call me "birthday girl" an embarrassing number of times. Then they all go back to making plans for the big celebration.

"Mother said she'd come by for us—Hank, Wes, and me—about noon," Popeye explains. "Then hopefully, we'll see you at the parade. But if we miss you, we'll meet at the Made-Rite at five."

"Works for me," Annie says. She gets up when I sit down. "Dakota, I'll be back no later than two o'clock. Three at the latest. Tell Kat to be ready, okay?" She dumps her dishes in the sink and looks around for her purse.

"Where *is* Kat?" Now that I know she's so sick, I worry every time she's not where she's supposed to be.

"Still looking for her kitten," Hank answers.

Wes reaches down and pets his dog. "I didn't do it on purpose." He gets up from the table and goes outside. Rex follows him.

"Sure hope that kitten comes back soon," Popeye says. "That cat means the world to her."

I don't want to sit with them any longer and pretend I don't know what's wrong with Kat. And I don't want to talk to them about it either. "I'm not hungry."

I find Kat in the barn, peering behind hay bales. "Kat?"

"Where would Kitten hide? Where would she want to make a new home?" She swipes at her eyes with the back of her hand, and I know she's been crying.

"Come on," I say. "There are some great places to hide in this barn."

Together, we search every corner of the hayloft and every stall. We find 11 barn cats but no trace of Kitten.

We move to the pasture behind the barn and conduct a row-by-row search for the rest of the morning. We're at the far end of the pasture when a horn honks.

Kat glances at her watch. "That's probably Gram for Wes and Hank and Daddy."

"And me." I can't look her in the eyes, so I gaze toward the honking car. "I decided to go with them."

"Why?" Kat sounds so disappointed.

But I can't stop now. "There are some people your dad wants me to meet. At the firehouse, I guess."

"That's nice," she says.

"You keep looking, Kat. Tell your mom I went with your dad, okay?" I take off running toward the house. But when I'm sure Kat's not watching, I circle back to the barn and duck in.

That's where I stay until I hear the car drive off. And that's where I stay for the next three hours, until Annie returns.

I keep out of sight until I hear Annie and Kat come out of the house, get in the van, and drive off, leaving me alone.

It was almost too easy.

When I'm sure they're really gone, I venture out and take another look around the barn for Kitten. I don't want Kat to come home and find her kitten still missing. The kid's going through enough. I check the tack room and stalls again, but the cat's nowhere.

Blackfire stamps the floor of his stall. He

nickers, and I take him a handful of oats. He eats out of my open palm, and his muzzle is softer than silk.

"I'm sorry I'm leaving you, Blackfire. But you're going to be fine. Hank will find you a great home. Whoever gets you will be the luckiest person in the world."

Finished with the oats, Blackfire lifts his head to nuzzle my nose. He exhales his warm breath into my face. I love this horse. My throat burns with the tears I'm swallowing. I press my cheek against his and inhale, memorizing his horsey scent.

I want to remember everything we've done together. Even the rough times, like when he ran away with me clinging to his mane, not sure if I loved it or hated it. We're so much alike. Fight or flight. That about sums up my life.

Something nags at me when I think about the phrase. *Fight or flight.*

"Blackfire, that's it! Why didn't I think of this before? Kitten chose *flight*!" She's not in the barn. She's not hiding. She was scared, and she ran. If anybody understands runaways, it's me. Kitten didn't run *to* anything. She ran *away*.

EIGHTEEN

IN TWO MINUTES, I've bridled Blackfire. Mounting him is a bigger problem. I manage to lead him close enough to the fence for me to climb up on him. He doesn't move until I'm square on his back.

"Come on, boy." I lean forward and grip with my thighs. In less than an hour, Neil will be here. I have to find Kitten and bring her back first.

We walk out of the barn. The wind kicks up, and I grab a lock of Blackfire's mane. "Let's find Kitten," I murmur. Sensing he understands,

I lay the reins across his neck, turning him west, toward the quarry.

As I squeeze in with my thighs, Blackfire breaks into a canter that turns to a gallop. I lean forward, almost on his neck. His mane whips me in the face, tickling my cheeks. I let him go, just like the day he ran away with me. Only this time we're both running *to* something. We have to find Kitten. Kat deserves that much from me, at least.

Hooves pound the hard ground, and my heart beats in rhythm to the *thud thump, thud thump*. A woodpecker knocks somewhere above us. The eerie cry of a mourning dove lingers in the breeze. It's music I can feel in my soul, like Popeye said the day I arrived and heard my first woodpecker. God's knocking at the soul.

I don't know if I've ever felt love before, but I feel it now. Blackfire's love. And maybe something more. Much more.

We gallop across the road. I imagine Kitten running like this, scared, running away. This is how she'd run. I know it. Run like crazy, not looking back.

We're close to the quarry. Wind presses

against me from all sides, wraps me in its arms, like a giant hug. I wish I could hold on to it. The verse Kat told me was her favorite floats at the edges of my mind. Something about God loving us so much that He calls us His children. And again I wonder what that would be like— to be God's child, part of a family, loved.

At the edge of the quarry, Blackfire stops. I slide off and drop his reins to the ground. "Stay," I tell him. And I trust him not to leave me. Not to run away.

"Here, Kitten!" I step along the edge of the quarry, calling, but there's no sign of her. So I pray. "God . . ." Only I stop. I've shot off a wish-prayer before in times like this. But it's not enough. Not now. Things feel different.

I'm different. "God, thank You for letting me live with this family, even for a short time. I'll never forget them or the love I saw here. I know You love Kat. And You've gotta know how much she loves this kitten. Please, God. Please help me find it. And I'm sorry to be asking You like this again. But I know You care about this. Kat's Your kid."

I drop to my stomach and peer over the edge of the quarry. Behind me, Blackfire snorts.

Thunder rumbles in the distance. "Kitten? Where are you?"

Then I see her. She's curled up in the crook of a rock about a foot below. Tiny cries float up to me. "It's okay, Kitten."

I stretch as far as I can without falling into the quarry. My fingers dangle above the cat. But I can't reach her. "Stand up, Kitten. Please?" *Please, God! For Kat? For me?*

And then I feel something soft. Furry. Kitten's standing. Her back arches, and I slide my hand under her belly and lift her up.

Hanging on to the cat, I scoot away from the ledge. When we're safe, I pull Kitten to my chest and hug her the way Kat does. "Thank You." Tears are streaming down my face. Kitten purrs. "I'm taking you home."

Blackfire is right where I left him. I find a big rock to stand on so I can mount. Kitten curls in front of me as I take the reins. "Slow and easy, boy," I whisper.

With one hand cradling Kitten and the other holding the reins, I can't grab my security handful of mane. But I don't need to. Blackfire understands. His walk is rocking-chair smooth as we make our way home.

Home. But it's not home. Not *my* home. And Neil could be there right now, ready to take me away.

We reach the road, and the roof of the farmhouse rises through the clouds in the distance. The rumbles of thunder grow louder.

A horn honks. Blackfire jerks to a stop. I struggle to keep from falling off. Kitten cries and tries to jump off.

When I regain my balance, I glare at the honking car.

It's Neil. He's in the passenger seat of a light blue convertible, the top down. DJ's behind the wheel.

"Neil?" I ride closer. "You actually came." This is what I've wanted since the day I left Chicago. Neil has come to take me away.

"What, you turned into a cowgirl?" Neil bursts into a laugh that scares Kitten. "How about trading that thing in for something with wheels?"

DJ turns down the radio, which seems loud and out of place. "We don't have all day, man. Let's get out of here."

"Sure," I answer. "I just need to take this cat back and leave a note for the Coolidges."

"We don't have time, Dakota," Neil says, glancing at DJ.

"It won't take long." I can't abandon Kitten. I don't expect Neil to understand.

"Put it down. Don't they always find their way home, like pigeons?" Neil laughs and makes DJ laugh too.

"I can't, Neil. It's a runaway."

"So let it run. Doesn't seem like it wants to go home anyway." Neil's voice has an edge to it, like he's running out of patience fast.

"I'm taking it home," I insist. "I have to get the horse back in the barn anyway."

DJ shakes his head. "We don't have time for this, man."

Neil glances over his shoulder and down the road. He looks nervous, almost scared. "What's with you, Dakota?"

"Nothing." I force a smile. I've known Neil for a long time. He drove all this way to get me. He cares about me. "Nothing's wrong with me. I just have to get my stuff is all. So I might as well take the cat and the horse back there." I urge Blackfire to take a step.

"Forget that!" Neil shouts. "Get in." He opens the front door and scoots over. "We can drive to the house, and you can run in and get your stuff, okay?"

Is it? Is it okay? I've only known the Coolidges a couple of weeks. Still, I can't just take off. I don't want to have Kat come home and find her kitten . . . *and* me . . . gone. And what am I supposed to do with Blackfire?

"Come on!" Neil snaps. "You don't owe those people anything."

But I do. I see that more clearly than I've ever seen anything. I do owe them.

Neil's jaw tightens, and he swears. "Get in the car right now!"

"I can't, Neil." My stomach is squeezing together. I feel Blackfire tense beneath me.

Neil glances at DJ, and I think he's trying to decide if he should tell me something. "Dakota, we have to get out of state fast."

"Why?"

DJ slaps the steering wheel. "I'm out of here, man!"

"Dakota?" Neil's voice is softer now, almost pleading.

Blackfire paws the ground. He wants to go home. *Home.*

My head starts shaking no before my

mind tells it to. "No," I whisper. When I say it, my stomach untwists.

Blackfire stops pawing. Kitten purrs. I hear a woodpecker somewhere, and it makes me smile. Then Blackfire whinnies soft and low. And it's all like secret music, soul music, as if God's striking up His orchestra to draw me to Him, into His family.

Neil slams the car door shut. "Suit yourself." His voice is sharp, cruel even. "What happened to you, Dakota?"

It's a fair question. Something *has* happened to me. "Love," I answer simply.

"Great. Why didn't you tell me you had a guy out here?" Neil sounds angry but not hurt.

I let out a little laugh. "I don't, Neil." And the thought hits me that it's God's love. I'm amazed at this thought.

Neil looks at me as if I've grown another head.

DJ revs the engine. "I'm not giving her money back."

I've never been sorrier for anything than I am about taking that money. I'll work and give back every cent. Still, Popeye's right. There's so much I can't pay back. "Bye, Neil."

They peel out, leaving us in a cloud of dirt and dust. Still Blackfire and Kitten are as calm as I've ever seen them.

And the crazy thing is, so am I. I've just sent away my best chance at running away. I've cut myself off from the only friend I've had for years. Yet I'm purring inside, just like Kat's kitten. If I could nicker, I would. Blackfire and Kitten aren't the only ones going home. So am I.

When I reach the driveway, I see the van parked on the lawn. Hank comes running up the drive. "Dakota!" He turns around and yells toward the house. "She's back!"

Popeye and Annie come running from the house, with Wes behind them.

Hank's grandmother and Kat are holding hands. Kat breaks away and races to me. "Dakota!" She's crying, and I feel rotten for putting her through this.

I hold out her kitten. "Look who I found."

"Kitten!" she cries. She reaches up and takes the cat from me, then buries her face in the fur. "How . . . ? Where did you find her?"

"Once I figured out that she ran away, it was pretty easy. She was at the quarry."

Tears are covering her cheeks and dripping

onto her kitten. "I thought you were both gone forever."

Hank takes Blackfire's reins. "Were you going to run away on Blackfire?"

"How'd you know I'd run away?"

Popeye glances behind him at Wes. "Soon as we got to the Made-Rite and you weren't there, we figured out you'd told me you were riding with Annie, and Annie you were riding with me. Wes said we'd better come back here and stop you because you were planning to run away."

I stare at Wes, amazed he'd want to stop me.

Wes smiles at me and shrugs. "So maybe I'm not as ready to get rid of you as I made out, okay?"

"Okay," I answer.

"Dakota, why would you run away?" Popeye asks.

I look at him and at Annie, and I know I have to get it all out. "Running away is the only thing I know how to do," I admit. But I can't stop here. "I took money from your pet bowl." I wait. And I wonder if they'll yell at me, if they'll tell me to go ahead and run away.

Annie grins at Popeye, then at me. "Oh, honey, we knew that."

"You did?" I'm amazed. "You didn't say anything."

"We don't care about the money," Popeye says. "We figured you'd tell us why you took it when you were ready."

"I sent it to Neil, my friend in Chicago, so he could drive here and get me. We were going to Los Angeles."

"*Were?*" Hank asks.

"He still is," I answer. "I told him I'm not going. I sent him away."

"Yes!" Popeye says.

"Way to go, Dakota!" Kat exclaims.

"But he took your money with him. I'll pay it back," I add quickly. "Every penny. And I know you might not even want me around now, but I'll still pay you back. I promise."

"Don't be silly!" Annie says. "How could we not want you to stay in your own home?"

"Does anybody realize that she's riding my wild horse? However did she manage that?" Popeye's mother keeps her distance in her lacy dress and sequined hat.

"Isn't it wonderful, George?" Annie exclaims.

"George?" I repeat. Something clicks. "Did you just call her George?"

"Georgette Amelia on my birth certificate," she explains. "Annie is the only person I allow to call me George, so don't get any ideas."

"I knew George before I knew her charming son," Annie explains, winking at her husband.

George. "Then you're the one who sent the e-mail? You're the one who said you had to meet her? that you loved her and missed her?" How could I have been so stupid?

Annie bursts out laughing. "Dakota! Did you read my e-mail? Now it all makes sense. You thought George was a man!"

Sheepishly I nod.

"And that's why you hung up on my boss?" Annie says, between chokes of laughter.

I nod again. "Sorry."

"Hey!" Kat cries, shifting Kitten to one arm and digging into her pocket with her free hand. "Don't forget it's a happy birthday around here." She hands me something wrapped in white tissue paper.

I unwrap it, trying to remember the last birthday gift I got.

It's a tiny plaque of rough barn wood. Somebody's burned into the wood:

See how very much our Father loves us, for he calls us his children, and that is what we are!
1 JOHN 3:1

"Hank did the wood burning," Kat says. "It's from both of us."

"And me," Wes claims.

I look around me—at Kat and Hank, Wes, Annie and Popeye, and "George." And I think I believe this verse. Because for the first time in my life, I'm getting it—love, family, the whole forgiveness thing. I don't understand all of it. But there'll be time. I'm not going anywhere.

"Look!" Wes shouts, pointing to the sky. "They're starting."

"Fireworks!" Kat squeals.

"George" pulls blankets from her trunk and sets them out so we can watch the Nice fireworks. Instead of putting Blackfire back in the barn, Hank lets me keep him out with us. Rex watches too, and Taco and Kitten.

This is how Ms. Bean and her fiancé find

us when they drive up. We scoot together to make room for them and watch the fireworks burst in a sky that has cleared just for us. Together, we shout "ooh" and "aah" at the same time, like we've rehearsed it.

I settle back, with Blackfire at my head and this new family all around me, as fireworks explode across the sky. I'm not leaving. No fight, no flight. And for the first time in a very long time, I feel like I really do have something to celebrate.

Tips on Finding the Perfect Pet

- Talk with your whole family about owning a pet. Pets require a commitment from every member of the family. Your pet should be around for years—ten, fifteen, twenty, twenty-five, or thirty years, depending on the type of pet. Pets can be expensive, especially if they get sick or need medical care of any kind. Make sure you can afford to give your pet a good life for a long time.

- Think like your future pet. Would you be happy with the lifestyle in your house? Would you spend most of your time alone? Is there room for you in the house? If you're considering buying a horse, what kind of life will the horse have? Will someone be able to spend enough time caring for it?

- Study breeds and characteristics of the animal you're considering. Be prepared to spend time with your pet, bonding and training, caring and loving.

- Remember that there is no such thing as a perfect pet, just as there's no such thing as a perfect owner. Both you and your pet will need to work to develop the best possible relationship you can have and to become lifelong best friends.

Consider Pet Adoption

- Check out animal rescue organizations, such as the humane society (www.hsus.org), local shelters, SPCA (www.spca.com), 1-800-Save-A-Pet.com (PO Box 7, Redondo Beach, CA 90277), Pets911.com (great horse adoption tips), and Petfinder.com. Adopting a pet from a shelter will save that pet's life and make room for another animal, who might also find a good home.

- Take your time. Visit the shelters and talk with the animal caregivers. Legitimate shelters will be able to provide you with documentation on the animal's health and medical records. Find out all you can. Ask questions. Who owned the pet before? How many owners were there? Why was the pet given away? Is the pet housebroken? Does it like children?

- Consider adopting an adult pet. People tend to favor the "babies," but adopting a fully grown animal may be less risky. What you see is what you get. The personality and size and manners are there for you to consider.

Rescuing Animals

- It's great that you want to help every animal you meet. I wish everyone felt the same. But remember that safety has to come first. A frightened, abused animal can strike out at any time. If you find an animal that's in trouble, call your local animal shelter. Then try to find the owner.

- The best way to help a lost pet find its home again is to ask around. Ask friends, neighbors, classmates, the newspaper deliverer, and the mail carrier. You might put a "Found Pet" ad in the paper or make flyers with the animal's picture on it. But be sure to report the find to your local shelter because that's where most owners will go for help in finding a lost pet.

- Report animal cruelty to your local animal shelter, to the humane society, or to organizations like Pets911 (www.pets911.com/services/animalcruelty).

AUTHOR TALK

DANDI DALEY MACKALL grew up riding horses, taking her first solo bareback ride when she was three. Her best friends were Sugar, a Pinto; Misty, probably a Morgan; and Towaco, an Appaloosa. Dandi and her husband, Joe; daughters, Jen and Katy; and son, Dan, (when forced) enjoy riding Cheyenne, their Paint. Dandi has written books for all ages, including Little Blessings books, *Degrees of Guilt: Kyra's Story, Degrees of Betrayal: Sierra's Story, Love Rules, Maggie's Story,* and the best-selling series Winnie the Horse Gentler. Her books (about 450 titles) have sold more than 4 million copies. She writes and rides from rural Ohio.

Visit Dandi's Web site at
www.dandibooks.com

S✦T✦A✦R✦L✦I✦G✦H✦T

Animal Rescue

More than just animals need rescuing in this new series. Starlight Animal Rescue is where problem horses are trained and loved, where abandoned dogs become heroes, where stray cats become loyal companions. And where people with nowhere to fit in find a place to belong.

#1 *Runaway* – *available now!*

#2 *Mad Dog* – *available now!*

#3 *Wild Cat* – *coming spring 2009*

#4 *Dark Horse* – *coming spring 2009*

Read all four to discover how a group of teens cope with life and disappointment.

WWW.TYNDALE.COM/KIDS

CP0264

Can't get enough of Winnie? Visit her Web site to read more about Winnie and her friends plus all about their horses.

IT'S ALL ON WINNIETHEHORSEGENTLER.COM

There are so many fun and cool things to do on Winnie's Web site; here are just a few:

⭐ PAT'S PETS

Post your favorite photo of your pet and tell us a fun story about them

⭐ ASK WINNIE

Here's your chance to ask Winnie questions about your horse

✦ MANE ATTRACTION

Meet Dandi and her horse, Cheyenne!

⭐ THE BARNYARD

Here's your chance to share your thoughts with others

✦ AND MUCH MORE!